DAMAGE CONTROL

THE BILLIONAIRE'S MUSE BOOK 4

M. S. PARKER

BELMONTE PUBLISHING, LLC

This book is a work of fiction. The names, characters, places and incidents are products of the writer's imagination or have been used fictitiously and are not to be construed as real. Any resemblance to persons, living or dead, actual events, locales or organizations is entirely coincidental.

Copyright © 2017 Belmonte Publishing LLC

Published by Belmonte Publishing LLC

ISBN-13: 978-1983422584

ISBN-10: 1983422584

NOTE FROM M. S. PARKER

Thank you so much for reading Damage Control, the last book in Billionaire's Muse, a series about four different Doms from Gilded Cage. All four books can be read stand-alone, but I recommend reading them in the following order:

> The Billionaire's Muse
> Bound
> One Night Only
> Damage Control

As a secret surprise, I'm writing a bonus novella, Change of Plans (The Billionaire's Muse – The Wedding). I'm not telling who's wedding we'll attend, but everybody will be there, so be sure you are signed up to my newsletter and I'll email the ebook to you for free, TWO WEEKS

BEFORE the official release on Amazon on Valentine's day. Go to www.msparker.com/Newsletter to sign up for the free pre-release ebook copy of the book.

M. S. Parker

ONE
PAIGE

I loved my mom. Really, I did, but I was never letting her choose a restaurant again. Not for a Sunday brunch, or a Saturday dinner.

Nothing.

Ever.

Again.

In every aspect of her life since my birth, she chose the boring, predictable route...except when it came to selecting restaurants. Instead of picking a nice Italian place or maybe Thai, Cuban, Japanese, she always went for the odd ones out. The restaurants with gimmicks or strange menus.

Like the place in the Bronx last year that tried to do pizza stir-fry with BBQ sauce. Or the one that used stationary bikes instead of tables and chairs so that people could burn off calories while they ate.

This one, however, was the last straw, and I made sure she knew it.

"Never again, Mom." I glared at her across the table. "I mean it."

She smiled at me, and not for the first time, I wondered if people thought we were sisters rather than mother and daughter. She'd been twenty-two when I was born, but even now, she barely looked ten years older than me. We had the same raven-black hair, though I wore my long and she kept hers at chin-length. My blue eyes had some green in them, while hers were pure, pale blue. Other than those small details, the two of us looked so much alike that it was occasionally creepy.

"You work too hard," she said. "You need to have some fun."

I raised an eyebrow. "Really? *That's* your excuse for bringing me here? I'm going to have nightmares for months."

Mom laughed, but the sound was drowned out as the next act took the stage. Karaoke was bad enough, but a restaurant that awarded prizes for the worst karaoke possible? That was just evil.

I dipped a French fry into some ranch dressing and popped it into my mouth. At least the food was good. One place we'd gone a few weeks back had only served things that tasted like cardboard. At least what I assumed cardboard would taste like. I'd had to pick up a pizza on the way home.

I winced as someone attempted to hit a high note. I didn't know how Mom could listen to this, especially when I knew how she felt about pop and 'adult contemporary' music. Unlike some of my school friends' parents, my mom hadn't forbidden me to listen to rock music. In fact, she'd encouraged it, sharing her favorites before I could speak.

She'd never hidden her past from me. I couldn't even remember the first time she told me about how she'd followed bands around the country from age fifteen until she'd gotten pregnant with me, but it was young enough that, no matter how much I loved her, I'd always known that I didn't want to repeat her life.

Which was why, even though she'd never been overly permissive or overly strict, I'd always been a good kid. No partying, no drugs or drinking, no sex, no late nights. I worked. First at school, then college, and now my job.

Except this horrific rendition of "My Heart Will Go On" was making me feel more than a little rebellious.

"I can't take another song," I said as soon as the song ended. "Please."

Mom sighed good-naturedly and nodded. I didn't give her a chance to change her mind and waved over the waiter, a tanned, blond athlete who looked like he'd be more at home on a California beach than a restaurant in New York City. He came over almost immediately, which wasn't surprising since he'd been staring at me almost from the moment we'd walked in.

"Check, please," I practically shouted to be heard.

When he came back five minutes later, his cheeks were flushed, and from the way his eyes kept darting to the bill, it didn't take a genius to figure out that he'd either left a note asking for my phone number...or left me his. I wasn't about to encourage him, so I slipped a couple bills into the fold without looking inside. I'd done enough of the math in my head to know I'd covered the cost of the meal and given him a nice tip.

"Keep the change," I said with a polite smile. I turned to my mom before I could see any disappointment on the young man's face.

It wasn't anything personal. He was handsome and seemed nice enough. The sort of guy that most women would love to have hitting on them, but I wasn't most women. Finding a man wasn't high on my priority list. It wasn't on it at all, actually. Not for dating, marrying, or fucking.

I didn't hate men. I just didn't need one. Not at this point in my life, and maybe not ever. I had enough on my plate without adding the complication of a relationship. Hell, I'd never met anyone worth the hassle of a one-night stand.

I blew out a breath and twisted my hair up behind my head in preparation for stepping out into the late August heat. As a native New Yorker, I was accustomed to the city summers, but I always preferred the city in the winter. Sure, the sidewalks could be downright dangerous at times, but I'd take cold over hot any day.

"Next time, we're going to Maialino," I said as we made our way to the subway.

Although I wasn't rich, I made enough money that I could have rented us a car, but this was part of our tradition too. Sometimes, we missed a Sunday or two because life got in the way, but when we did go, we had a certain way of doing things. Taking the subway back to the apartment where I'd grown up so we could have dessert was part of it.

"That's not very special," Mom said.

I gave her a sideways look. "Your idea of a special place to eat and mine are definitely *not* the same."

As we turned the corner, she changed the subject, but not to something new. "You've been working a lot of overtime lately."

I nodded. "Ms. Feldt has been giving me more responsibility now that I'm done with school."

She pushed a few strands of hair from her face as she looked at me with concern. "You've only been out of school since May. Shouldn't she be easing you into things?"

"I don't want to be eased into things," I said, fighting to keep the irritation out of my voice. We'd had this discussion a dozen times since I graduated. "I *like* my job. I *like* working."

I didn't have to look at her to know she was giving me the same skeptical look she'd given me every other time we'd had similar discussions over the years. Mom had worked hard to raise me on her own, but she only saw work as something she needed to do, never something she wanted to do. She didn't understand that I did what I did because I *wanted* to. No matter how similar we were in many ways, I wasn't like her.

"Speaking of work," I continued, "how are things going for you in that department?"

"Same as always." She shrugged, her mouth growing tight at the corners. "It's a job."

"You know, you could go to college, pursue a career of your choosing." We picked a place on the platform and waited. "Now that I'm done, it could be your turn."

Her smile was soft, but she looked past me, not at me. "There's really no point. I've never had anything that I've really wanted to do. Nothing I wanted to be. Other than a mom, of course."

Sometimes, I thought she actually believed it when she said that, but I'd spent too many years hearing the happiness in her voice when she talked about being on the road with all those bands. If I hadn't come along, she probably would've ended up being a manager and never settled down. I knew she didn't resent me for it, but there were times I wondered if she found herself missing the life she'd missed.

"You know that I just want you to be happy," Mom said as we moved onto the subway car.

I forced a bright smile. "I am happy."

She gave me a skeptical look but didn't argue with me. She didn't need to. We'd had this discussion before. She meant well, I knew, but like a lot of parents, she just didn't get how different the two of us really were from each other. She loved me, I never doubted that, but she didn't *get* me.

Even as I thought it, she reached over and gave my hand a squeeze. "Why don't you tell me about your latest project?"

TWO
REB

I groaned as I came back to consciousness after several blissful hours of nothing. I did this because I wanted to forget, but nothing came without a cost, and I was feeling that right now.

My head felt like I had an iron spike going through one temple and out the other, a sharp, pulsing pain that I knew would only get worse when I opened my eyes. My mouth was dry and tasted like some wild animal had taken a shit in it. I could smell the alcohol leaking from my pores, and with it, I registered sweat and sex.

No surprises there.

I'd started drinking pretty much the moment I'd caught my ex cheating on me nearly three months ago, and I'd been hooking up with random women two or three times a week for almost that same period of time. I didn't remember much about last night, but I knew it hadn't been much different than the previous ones.

Finally, I forced my eyes open, wincing reflexively even though the curtains were all closed. The room was dark, but I didn't need to see to know that I was in a hotel, probably the one I'd been practically living in since the cheating girlfriend incident. I'd kicked her out of my apartment, and I still paid my rent every month, but I hadn't been able to stop seeing her fucking other men in my bed every time I walked into the bedroom. I'd replaced the bed, but that hadn't helped.

Nothing helped except drowning myself in women and alcohol. And even that didn't help for long.

I rolled toward the edge of the bed, prepared to stagger my way into the bathroom and take a shower, half to avoid having an awkward morning-after conversation, and half because I stunk. It was part of the new routine that had become my shitty life.

But I couldn't climb out of bed the way I usually did because someone was in the way.

I frowned and turned the other way, but there was a body on that side too. A flash of memory from last night went through my mind.

A blonde and a redhead knelt on either side of me, both wearing black silk thongs and nothing else. The blonde was nibbling my ear, her breasts pressing against my arm, and her friend was leaning over my lap, her tongue moving over my cock like it was some sort of fucking lollipop.

Another immediately followed.

The red-head smiled up at me, her eyes half-lidded,

pupils so dilated that I knew she was on something other than the tequila shots we'd done together. That was her business though. My business was fucking the blonde who was stretched on the bed between the redhead's legs, eating out the pussy I'd be fucking next.

I scratched my head, then resigned myself to crawling to the foot of the bed so I could get up without waking either of the women hidden under the covers. I'd apparently enjoyed their company last night, but I wasn't interested in things carrying over to this morning.

When I reached the bathroom, I braced myself for the light, but it didn't prevent me from grimacing at the reflection in the mirror. My eyes were bloodshot, but I could take care of that with a pair of sunglasses. Being a rock star came with the sort of perks that included being able to wear sunglasses anywhere, anytime, without being called a douche.

I took a piss while I let the shower heat up, then let out a stream of curses when I stepped under the spray. One of those women had scratched the hell out of my back.

By the time I was done, I felt cleaner, but not really any better. I tossed back a couple aspirin and swallowed them with a full glass of water. Hydration would help me feel at least a bit more human, and hair of the dog was always good for a hangover. One of the best parts about having access to an obscene amount of money was that I didn't have to think twice about cleaning out the mini bar. I could afford it.

As soon as I stepped out of the bathroom, I was doubly glad for the fact that I had money. The women were gone, and as far as I could tell, they hadn't stolen anything. Unfortunately, as the now-blazing lights revealed, it was most likely because they couldn't find anything in the mess.

Shit.

I remembered drinking, and I remembered pieces of fucking both women, but I didn't remember trashing the room. I didn't doubt that I'd done it though. I'd apparently cleared out the mini-bar already because at least a dozen tiny bottles were all over the place. Two ceramic lamps and what looked like every vase and bowl in the place had been shattered into hundreds of pieces. It was a fucking miracle that we hadn't cut our feet walking through here.

This was going to be pricey.

And then I saw that we'd somehow managed to destroy both the television and a chair. I didn't bother keeping the curses inside my head this time.

My manager was going to have my ass if this ended up being as bad as it looked, and something nagging in the back of my mind told me it was actually worse.

I picked my way back into the bedroom to find clothes and my phone. Whatever was nagging at the back of my brain, it'd be on my phone. Once I figured that out, I'd call the front desk and see about getting someone up here to clean things up. I'd make a healthy donation above and beyond what I'd be charged for damage done.

And then I'd find myself something to take the edge off.

As soon as I found my phone, I saw half a dozen voicemails from Chester waiting. And a calendar reminder about an important recording appointment that I'd missed by more than ninety minutes.

"Fuck me," I muttered. I was going to need more than just a small drink.

I put the phone on speaker and let the voicemails play through while I grabbed some clothes.

"Reb, you're late. You better have a damn good excuse, or you'll have a shitload of explaining to do."

"Where the hell are you, kid? He ain't going to wait around forever."

"Fuck it, Reb! You better be dead because anything short of that won't be excuse enough."

They went on like that, each one a little louder and with considerably more expletives. If Chester was already this pissed off, he was going to be livid when he found out about the hotel room.

Then came the last voicemail, the one I hadn't noticed but wished I would have seen first.

"Reb, this is your mother, in case you're currently too drunk to recognize my voice. I don't know what's gotten into you as of late, but I expect you to be at the Union Square Ballroom this evening or we will be having a serious discussion about your priorities."

A rush of guilt washed over me.

Everyone had told my mom not to let me go into music,

and definitely not rock. I'd get into the whole sex and drugs lifestyle. I'd fuck my way through groupies and be lucky if my dick didn't fall off from some raging STD or get someone pregnant. I'd be drunk and high most of the time and have at least one overdose by the time I was twenty-five. I'd blow through everything I earned and then start on my inheritance, ending up broke and possibly homeless before forty. And that was being generous.

She'd silently told them all to go to hell by encouraging me. After my dad had died, music had become my escape, and she'd seen that. She'd told me that I had to apply to college and work on a degree, but if I landed a contract, I could quit school. I'd gotten into Columbia and majored in music education for two years, and then Chester Lhaw had found me. Mom had been true to her word and hadn't said a single word against it when I dropped out.

I'd worked my ass off, not just at proving I could make it in such a cutthroat business, but at making sure everyone saw that my mom had been right to put her faith in me. Despite my numerous tattoos and the bad boy image the studio crafted for me, I was as far from the stereotypical rock star as a person could get. No drugs. No all-night parties. No arrests. Discretion when it came to sexual partners.

Well, at least until recently.

I didn't need to hear my mother say how disappointed she was in me because I could hear it in her voice, and that was worse than my hangover.

I looked at the time and then pulled up my calendar to

double-check when I needed to be at the fundraiser. As much as I hated myself for it, I was going to need some liquid courage before I'd be able to face my mother.

I'D ONLY PLANNED on having one or two drinks before stepping into the ballroom. Just enough to take the edge off my headache and make fielding questions about my love life bearable. The kind of people who came to these charity events might have liked pretending that they were beyond such things as gossip, but they never had a problem asking me about the latest story as if I had the inside track to all of it.

Unfortunately, my break-up had made tabloid headlines for a couple weeks, and even though it happened in June, I knew there'd be people here who'd want to ask me about it. Plus, based on the looks I'd gotten from strangers already today, I had a bad feeling that word had gotten around about me trashing the hotel room last night.

With all of that in my head, I'd indulged in a bit more Four Roses than I should have, and now I found walking in a straight line to be a little problematic.

My mom's mouth flattened as I approached her, and as soon as I leaned down to kiss her cheek, she grabbed my arm.

"You came here drunk?" Her voice was barely a whisper, but I could hear her displeasure.

I straightened. "I'm fine."

She didn't have a chance to say anything else because the president of some arts foundation was coming toward us, and we didn't air our dirty laundry in public. I'd probably be in for it after the event, but for right now, I was safe. I gave people polite nods of acknowledgment as I made my way to the bar and ordered the most pretentious scotch they had.

I'd made it through my second glass when a pale, weedy-looking guy stepped up to the bar next to me. I was prepared to ignore him, but as soon as he downed his drink, he turned to me and started talking.

"You're the rock star, aren't you?" His voice was louder than it needed to be, which was infinitely more annoying than his question. "Mr. Hot Shot musician who lowers himself to come down and talk to the little people."

I pulled myself up to my full height, which was taller than most, and *much* taller than this guy, and glared down at him. "I think you should walk away and let me drink in peace."

His cheeks flushed, and a quick glance over his shoulder told me that he was trying to impress someone, but all that did was irritate me even more. I was not in the mood to deal with this.

"Why are you even here?" he asked, either the alcohol or the people watching us giving him the courage to say things he shouldn't. "You clearly don't fit in. Sure, you may have money, but it's not the kind that comes with class. The Whitehall name used to demand respect, but everyone here knows your mother lost it when she went slumming with some jarhead—"

Anything else he would've said was lost when my fist connected with his jaw, and he dropped to the floor, blood trickling from the corner of his mouth to pool on the polished wood.

Shit. That wouldn't go over well.

THREE
PAIGE

"Near, far, wherever... Fuck."

I wasn't sure if the elderly man in front of me shot me a dirty look because of the song or the curse. I'd caught myself humming that song all day yesterday, and I'd hoped it'd be out of my head by the time I got to work, but no such luck, apparently.

I slipped my earbuds in and turned the volume up almost loud enough to hurt. I didn't have anything against Celine Dion, but classical, and other instrumental pieces were my preference. The sort of music that didn't get much in the way of recognition.

By the time I got my Iced Caramel Macchiato, some Bach and Debussy had chased Dion out of my head. They also did wonders for calming my nerves, which was always important before I went to work. I hadn't been lying when I told my mom that I enjoyed my job, but that didn't mean it couldn't be stressful.

As the elevator doors opened, I took a slow breath, turned off my music, and focused on the job ahead. I was the youngest full-time associate at the public relations firm, and I wasn't naïve enough to think that everyone believed I deserve the position I'd gotten. I didn't actually care what people thought in the sense of needing their approval, but I'd be damned if I proved the doubters right.

I ignored the morning chatter as my co-workers swapped stories of the things they'd done over the weekend. Everyone had their own little group. The young singles who exchanged tales of dancing, drinking, and sex. The young marrieds who liked to talk about how wonderful their spouses were. The middle management men who were either trying to convince everyone that they were going to be moving up the corporate ladder soon, or that they were happy where they were because it gave them time to do all of the crazy things the twenty-somethings were doing. And then there were the women who either complained that they couldn't get ahead because the men were sexist or insisted that any woman who did manage to get ahead was sleeping with someone higher up.

I had neither the time nor the patience for office gossip. I didn't really care who was doing what with whom. I wasn't there to make friends, and even if I had been, I hadn't met anyone yet who I'd want to make an exception for. I wasn't a people person.

"Paige!"

I kept my face blank as I moved a bit faster. My boss didn't get a smile or a grimace. Depending on what mood she was in, either one could earn me a lecture. Sybil Feldt wasn't the easiest person to work with, but she let me do a lot more than the others like me got to do. Plus, I didn't have to put up with any of the sexual overtures that many of the other women dealt with.

"Good morning, Ms. Feldt," I said as I handed over her Caffé Corretto.

"Did you finish the notes from last week's meeting with Grover's Peanut Brittle?" She barely even looked at me as she sipped her drink, but that wasn't anything new. She wasn't a friend or a mentor. She was my boss, and I appreciated her brusque way of doing things.

"Yes, ma'am," I said as I logged into my computer. "I emailed you a copy and filed a hard copy."

"Did you come up with anything new?" She tucked a strand of barley-colored hair behind her ear.

"I caught something Mr. Grover said in passing," I replied. "A memory of his father coming home after working all day, exhausted, but still taking the time to sit with him and listen to him talk about his day. I think that could be the emotional hook. Nothing big and flashy, but simple and family-focused."

To my surprise, she actually looked at me, hazel eyes shrewd. "That's a great idea."

"Do you want me to write up a proposal?" I kept my voice even. If I could get a proposal to even be considered for a major project like Grover's, it would go a long way to getting me a client of my own. Not something like repackaging the image of an entire company. Something simple, but mine all the same.

"Yes, type that up first thing. Once you get it done, I'll want to see you in my office."

Something about her tone made me look up at her, but she'd already gone. I finished up the sentence I was typing, sent off the email, and then hurried after her.

As soon as I was inside, she started talking.

"You know music, don't you?"

I stiffened, unable to stop myself. I didn't talk about my personal life at work. No one here knew who my mother was, or the story behind who I was. My mom had been a groupie for several years, but it wasn't like that was something she put on her résumé.

"Why would you think that?"

Sybil rolled her eyes. "You're young. Don't you keep music available like twenty-four seven?"

The hand squeezing my lungs eased, and I could breathe again. "I don't tend to listen to much in the way of popular music."

Again, a sideways look, this one with a raised eyebrow. "You might want to fix that."

I paused so I could make sure my voice was calm. "Is there a particular reason why, ma'am?"

"As a matter of fact, there is." She tossed her empty coffee cup into the trash. "You're getting your first assignment, and how well you do on it will determine where your career goes from here."

I should have been thrilled. This was exactly what I'd

wanted, what I'd been working my ass off for. Why I never questioned the fact that most of my job seemed to be doing Sybil's work for her.

Except my excitement was tempered by a sinking feeling in my stomach. "What's the assignment?"

"Ever hear of Reb Union?"

Shit.

"Yes, I have."

And I knew exactly why he was hiring a PR firm. He was everything I detested about most musicians, especially rock artists. Pretending to be some upstanding guy until something finally led to the curtain being pulled away to reveal that he was exactly like all the rest, caring only about partying.

And my job would be to hide all that shit, so he came out like some repentant creative genius who'd never do anything like that again.

FOUR
REB

I considered turning my phone off when I got home. I'd barely missed getting arrested after knocking out the son of a senator, and I knew my mother smoothing things over was the only reason I wasn't cooling off in a jail cell. I also knew I was going to hear it at some point today.

That was the reason why I'd kept it on. If I turned it off or sent her to voicemail, she wouldn't think twice about showing up at my apartment, and for the first time in months, I was actually there. After what I'd done to the hotel room, I knew better than to try to go back there, so I'd gone home.

But I'd slept on the couch. I'd told myself it was because I didn't want to chance throwing up on the bed, but that was only a half-truth. Even the guest room beds brought back memories of that night. For all I knew, she'd fucked guys on every bed in the apartment. Probably on the couch too, but it was easier to push that thought away because I hadn't caught her there. Not entirely logical, but it worked.

None of these things woke me up though. It was the jarring, shrill ringtone I'd assigned to my manager that pulled me out of a restless sleep.

"What?"

Shit, my voice sounded like I'd gargled with broken glass. I needed to be careful, or I wasn't going to have a career left to fuck up.

"What the hell, Reb?"

I put the phone on speaker and set it on the end table. If I was going to be treated to a lecture, at least I wouldn't have him yelling in my ear.

"First you flake out on an important meeting, and then I get a call from a hotel saying you and two women trashed their penthouse suite. They're claiming hundreds of thousands of dollars in damage."

"That's a bit much," I interrupted as I forced myself into a sitting position. "I cleaned out the mini-bar, but that wasn't exactly the finest quality alcohol."

He actually growled. "You broke the television, two lamps, two crystal vases, two crystal bowls, four wine glasses..."

He continued, reading from a list I assumed, and I put my head in my hands. It was sad, but I was almost used to waking up feeling like shit. I kept my eyes closed as I rubbed my temples, hoping to take enough of the edge off that I could walk without vomiting.

"The cleaning service also found three grams of coke in the bedroom."

I jerked my head up and immediately regretted it. "Wait, what?"

"Oh, *that* got your attention? Destruction of property, drunken disorderly, all that and you don't say a word, but some coke, and all of a sudden, you're the morality police?"

"Those aren't my drugs." I ignored his sarcasm. "You know I don't do that shit, Chester."

"I know you didn't *use* to do that shit," he countered. "You also never punched a senator's son during a charity event before last night either."

I scowled at the phone. "That's different. I don't do drugs. Hell, I barely drink."

As soon as the last sentence was out of my mouth, I knew he'd never believe that the drugs weren't mine. Because he was right. Up until recently, I'd never gotten so drunk that I couldn't control my impulses. Everything that had been true about my behavior before could be called into question now, and that included the drugs.

"I'll take a drug test," I offered. "Whatever you want me to do to prove that I'm clean."

"Nobody gives a shit if you can pass a drug test," Chester snapped. "There's ways around those things, and everyone knows it. It's what people think that's the problem now. Especially after the shit you pulled last night."

"He disrespected my parents." I was grateful to hear the words come out steady.

"You're nearly thirty years old, Reb," he said dryly. "And we both know that, no matter how good you are, music is no guaranteed future. We talked about this when you first signed with me. You get an image, and that gets you endorsement deals. That's what can set you up for life, even after everything else goes down the crapper."

I considered telling him that my inheritance was large enough that I could live a decent life off of interest alone, but I kept my mouth shut. I'd been with Chester for nearly a decade, and loyalty kept me with him, but I'd never trusted him enough to share certain things about myself, one of which was exactly how much money I had.

"What do my endorsement deals have to do with this?" I asked, suspecting I'd regret the question momentarily.

"You had a reputation as being clean, the sort of rock star who could be sold to families as someone safe for kids to admire."

I didn't miss the word *had*.

"One fucking screw-up and I'm suddenly on the same level as Ozzy Osbourne or Marilyn Manson?" I had nothing against those guys, but they weren't me.

"Ozzy's gone mainstream," Chester barked, his voice growing louder by the second. "And you've just proven to everyone that you're not as squeaky clean as you'd claimed."

I gritted my teeth to keep from reminding him that I hadn't billed myself as squeaky clean. I hadn't wanted to market myself as anything other than me from moment one, but Chester had sold me to the studio as someone who looked like a bad boy but behaved like the guy next door. I hadn't liked it, but they hadn't asked me to actually change who I was, so I'd just let it slide. It'd meant keeping certain preferences of mine a secret, but I'd always been a private guy when it came to that stuff. The people who mattered to me accepted me for who I was.

Or at least I'd thought they had until Mitzi had proven me wrong.

I pushed the thought of her out of my head as best I could.

"Can't you sell it as one day of bad choices? Come up with some sort of personal problem that got the better of me for twenty-four hours?" I hated myself for even asking it, but I had to ask.

"It hasn't been just twenty-four hours," he reminded me. "This was definitely the biggest mess you've made over the last couple months, but people have noticed a difference in you, and not a good one. Fans are either saying that you think you're too good for them, or that you're spiraling into depression, neither of which is great for your image. Anyone who's around you for more than a day notices that you're drinking all the time. You might not look or sound like you're drunk that much, but we can see the empty bottles and cans. You don't even try to hide it."

"I've had a shitty summer," I snarled, well aware that I sounded like the spoiled rich kid I promised myself I'd never become.

"Your girl cheated on you. Big fucking deal. If you'd listened to me in the first place, it wouldn't have been a problem. You can't get cheated on if you're not in a relationship."

"Well, I'm listening to you now," I countered. "Fucking random women without bothering to get their names, making sure they know where they stand."

"Yeah, well, a threesome with the niece of one of the studio heads and her friend wasn't exactly what I had in mind."

"Fuck," I muttered. I rubbed my hand over my jaw, trying to remember if either woman had told me that they were related to a bigwig where my contract was held. "I didn't know."

"You might have figured it out if you'd gotten your head out of your ass long enough to get sober enough to pay attention."

I stood and stretched. "Look, Chester, I'm expecting a call from my mom so she can lecture me on my bad behavior, so if that's all you're going to do, I'd like to get some coffee and a shower before I talk to her."

"That's not the main reason I called," he grouched, then sighed, loud and long. "I talked to the label this morning, and they've decided that you need to do damage control. I've already hired a PR firm, and they'll have someone over to see you first thing tomorrow."

"You hired someone without talking to me?" I was too tired to put much heat behind my words.

"I did. And you can fire her if you want, but if you do, there's a good chance the label's going to drop you."

I cursed under my breath but didn't argue. There was no point. Technically, I had a choice, but Chester and I both knew that I was stuck. I had to do what was expected of me or lose it all.

FIVE
PAIGE

I didn't want to do this.

I *really* didn't want to do this.

Most women would be thrilled at the chance to work with Reb Union. I'd never heard any of his music, but I doubted that was the draw. I'd seen enough pictures of him to know it wasn't just the money either. He had the sort of features that could only be described as pretty, and was six four, with an amazing body, and bronze hair that always looked like he'd just climbed out of bed. Added to that, the most uniquely colored irises I'd ever seen, and wow. Indigo. As in almost purple.

One of his endorsement deals was with a suit company, and someone on the marketing team had been absolutely brilliant. They'd had the color leached from everything except his eyes.

I might not like musicians – or most people, for that matter – but I wasn't a nun. He was gorgeous.

Not that it mattered. I knew better than to let a pretty face and hard body be anything more than fantasy fodder. The fact that he was a musician just made it easier to remember.

It hadn't been easy yesterday, not giving Sybil a list of reasons why this was a bad idea. If I had, she would've wanted to know why, and that wasn't anything I wanted to share, not with my boss, not with anyone. I loved my mother, and I was proud of everything she'd done to raise me on her own. I'd never let anyone say anything bad about her.

But that didn't mean I wanted to advertise the fact that she didn't know who my father was.

Just after she turned sixteen, she ran off to follow her boyfriend's band, but they'd broken up only a few weeks into the tour. Instead of going home, she'd moved on to a different member of a different band. For nearly six years, she gone from one musician to another, sometimes between a couple guys. Sometimes they shared her. She'd been into the whole sex, drugs, and rock 'n roll thing, never thinking about the future.

She'd always been honest about that, about why, and when she realized she was pregnant, she didn't have any way to figure out who my father was unless she asked for paternity tests. It hadn't mattered to her back then because she'd known that, whoever it was, he wouldn't want to be a father, and she'd never be able to count on him for any sort of support.

So, my father was either a washed-up wanna-be rock

god, or he'd actually managed to accomplish his dream, but either way, he wasn't the sort of man my mom had been able to count on. Which meant I'd learned young to not count on anyone other than myself and my mother.

"Are you going to get in the elevator, or just stand there, staring at it?"

The snide question pulled my attention back to the immediate present, and I managed not to scowl at the woman impatiently tapping her toe at me.

"Sorry about that," I offered as I stepped onto the elevator. That was the best she was going to get from me. I didn't appreciate getting a dirty look from someone who looked like she was doing a late walk of shame.

Her glare didn't get any friendlier when I pushed the button for the top floor. It was on the tip of my tongue to make up some lie about dating Reb, but I couldn't bring myself to even joke about it.

She got off on the seventh floor, and I rode the rest of the way up on my own. I didn't fall back into memories of my past though. No, I kept those firmly pushed down. This wasn't about me or my dislike of a particular group of people. This was work. I needed to be professional.

When I knocked on his door, I was focused and ready for anything.

Anything but realizing that Reb was better-looking in real life than he was in any of the pictures I'd seen.

He looked down at me, his eyes blood-shot and half-focused, then gave me one of those far-too-charming grins that guys like him seemed to master in the cradle.

"Mr. Union?" I bit back a moan at how lame I sounded. Like he was anyone else. "I'm Paige Ryce, your PR rep."

He stepped back from the door and made a sweeping gesture with one tattooed arm. I couldn't make out what the designs were without staring, so I ignored my curiosity and went inside.

"If I would've known I could order someone like you, I might not have been so pissed at Chester for doing it without asking."

I turned as he closed the door, folding my arms so I could give him a stern look. The alcohol fumes wafting off him were almost enough to make my eyes water. He was drunk. No surprise there.

"I'm here to discuss what my firm will do for you."

As soon as the words were out of my mouth, I regretted choosing them. His gaze narrowed in on me, something predatory in his eyes. I had to fight to stop from taking a step back. He wouldn't hurt me. That wasn't the underlying danger I saw. No, it was the kind that made my stomach twist.

"I can think of a whole lot of things that fine ass can do for me."

I raised an eyebrow. "How much have you had to drink today, Mr. Union?"

He gave me that grin again, the one that I knew he thought was so charming. "It's a compliment, Ms. Ryce."

"Today is just a preliminary meeting," I went back to the speech I'd originally planned. "We'll discuss the image issues we'll be working to correct, as well as any suggestions we can come up with to give us a place to start."

"Really?" He sauntered toward me with far more grace than an intoxicated person should have. "That's what you want to do? *Talk?* I can think of a lot of things that are more fun than talking."

If this was the way our conversations were going to go, I could think of a lot of things I'd rather be doing, but I wasn't going to take the bait. This might be a giant joke to him, but it wasn't to me. This was my job, my future, and I'd be damned if some drunken rock star ruined it for me.

SIX
REB

Full, pouting lips wrapped around my cock, and I buried my hand in her raven-black waves. Hair, soft as silk, slipped between my fingers, each lock in stark contrast to porcelain skin. Blue-green eyes looked up between thick lashes, desire visible in their ocean-like depths...

"Fuck me," I muttered as I flopped down on the couch.

I wrote notes and lyrics, not prose, but that didn't mean my imagination wasn't vivid enough to make me hard. And my imagination had been working overtime from the moment I opened my door to see my PR rep giving me a look full of enough disdain that I probably would've felt ashamed if the alcohol flowing through my body had allowed me to give a damn.

I didn't need a PR rep. I *shouldn't* need one. Wasn't everyone entitled to fuck up once in a while? I'd been in the music industry for nearly ten years, and all that time, I'd behaved myself. No scandals, no tabloid fodder beyond what the vultures made up. I showed up to things on time and always sober. I didn't have temper tantrums or make outrageous requests. I worked my ass off, and still found time to do charity work. I had casual sex, but it was always safe and consensual.

The only part of my life before this that could have caused issues, I made sure I kept private. Being into BDSM wasn't even really that shocking anymore. If I'd been a teacher or politician, the kind of guy parents wanted their children to emulate, sure, I'd understand. Even now, my sexual preferences wasn't something I wanted advertised, but it wasn't like I had some fucking morality clause in my contract that dictated what sort of sex I was allowed to like.

What had happened with Mitzi changed all of it. Everyone who'd gotten wind of the story had painted a sympathetic picture of me. At first.

Chester had made an agreement with Mitzi that I'd keep my mouth shut about certain aspects of the break-up if she did the same, but most fans figured out that Mitzi had cheated. I started losing sympathy points when my brooding over a beer or two became reclusive behavior with too much alcohol, especially when Mitzi seemed to be appropriately ashamed in public.

I understood that some poor choices over the weekend deserved head-shaking and finger-wagging, to use some of my mother's favorite phrases, but I could have done a lot worse things than trash a hotel room during a consensual threesome and punch a senator's son for making disparaging remarks about my dead father. The way I saw it, that incident was completely justified.

Okay, maybe I would've had a bit more self-control if I hadn't been drunk. But that didn't mean he deserved a punch any less.

I picked up my remote and turned on the TV, flipping through channels too fast to really see what was on. I wasn't much of a TV or movie watcher. Sometimes something would catch my interest, but I preferred music and reading. I hadn't been doing much of either recently though. Too much thought was involved in reading, and listening to music was a reminder of how little I'd written over the last six months.

I couldn't even blame that one on the break-up. I knew that part of the reason the studio had less patience with me than they would have in the past had to do with the fact that they had to keep pushing back the release date of my next album because I hadn't written anything beyond the first song. And that one was a steaming pile of bullshit.

I was still buzzed, walking a fine line between drunk and sober, but as everything piled up, reminding me of all the ways my life was fucked up at the moment, I wanted to get completely shit-faced. And why shouldn't I? I was in my apartment. If I wanted to get black-out drunk, whose business was it but mine? After all the times I'd made the smart, responsible choices, I deserved a break from dealing with my life.

I was still wallowing in self-pity and lethargy when someone knocked on my door.

For a moment, I thought Paige had come back, that my attempt at being flirtatious and charming had actually worked and she would let me lose myself in her body for a few blissful hours.

But then I remembered how disgusted she'd looked by the time she left. Disgusted...and relieved.

"Reb, open up! I have a key, but if you make me walk in on you naked again, I swear I'll take a picture and sell it to the highest bidder."

Erik.

Great.

I forced myself up and to the door. When I opened it, I saw it wasn't just Erik, but Jace and Alix too.

Even better.

"Come in," I said, not even bothering to try to curb my annoyance. "Shouldn't you all be living out your happily-ever-afters or whatever it is you do now?"

"Don't be an ass, Reb," Erik said mildly.

Sanders had been my college roommate at Columbia during the two years I'd gone there. I'd met his cousin one of the times Alix had come up to visit. The three of us had met Jace Randell at Gilded Cage, a club where people like us went to explore our desires without judgment.

These three were my closest friends, and in a lot of ways, they were closer to me than my own sisters. Each one was an artist of some kind. Jace was a painter slash sculptor. Alix, a photographer. Erik was the writer of the group. The four of us understood what it meant to think and create differently than most. If I told them that I was struggling with my music, they'd immediately know that it meant more than simply an issue with work. Because they'd all been there too.

Not now though, I remembered as I caught a glimpse of the ring on Alix's left hand. All three of them hadn't just found the loves of their lives recently, but also their muses. All of them were creating bigger and better things than they had before they'd met their soulmates.

Erik's newest book was flying off the shelves, and everyone wanted to know the real identity of Erika Summers. Being around him and his girlfriend, Tanya, was like having a front-row seat to the sappiest romantic comedy in the world.

Jace and his 'true love,' Savannah Birch, had another of those sickeningly sweet relationships, complete with overcoming odds. She'd woken up something in him, in his art, that I'd never seen before. His most recent show had been fantastic.

Then there was Alix. He'd just married his muse, Sine McNiven, even though she'd left him for more than a month without a word about where she'd gone or why she'd left. He hadn't been able to work the entire time she'd been gone, and the two of us had commiserated over our artistic block and the women responsible for them. Then she'd come back from Ireland, announced she was pregnant, and now the two of them were planning their nursery.

I was happy for them. Granted, the odds weren't exactly in their favor when it came to long-term happiness.

If they didn't crash and burn like most couples, then chances were they'd end up like my parents, with one outliving the other, always aware of that aching, bleeding emptiness where their other half had been. I hoped that my friends would make it work, that they'd build something lasting that wouldn't get their hearts broken in the end.

But I wasn't going to hold my breath.

"You look like shit," Jace said as the guys followed me back into my living room. "And so does your place. Don't you have a cleaning service?"

I shrugged and sat back down. "I canceled it for a while. Didn't want anyone bugging me."

"I figured that staying at a hotel would manage that," Alix said as he disappeared into the kitchen.

"You guys have been listening to the news." I made it a statement rather than a question.

"Is it wrong?" Erik asked, his expression serious. "Are they exaggerating?"

I reached for one of the beers Alix brought out, but he handed it to Erik instead. I glared at him, but answered Erik's question, "Depends on who's telling the story."

"You really punched Senator Mitchell's son in the middle of a fundraiser?" Alix chuckled.

Less than a month ago, Alix had been devastated, barely sleeping, drinking too much, and now he was laughing. He'd been as pathetic as I was, and I hadn't even loved Mitzi.

The revelation made me frown. I'd never actually

stopped to think about it, but it was the truth. She'd been my first serious girlfriend, the *only* serious one, and we'd been together for ten months before the shit hit the fan.

But I didn't love her. I hadn't *ever* loved her.

Which meant I couldn't blame a broken heart for what I'd been doing.

Shit.

Before I could become too introspective, Alix spoke, "Look, I'm not going to bust your balls. I've been there. But if you miss my show this weekend, or you come in wasted, I'm going to kick your ass."

I didn't need to look at him to know he was serious. I nodded slowly. "Fair enough."

Erik leaned forward. "All right, Reb, let's cut the shit. This has been going on long enough. You need to get your act together."

I stared at him for a moment before laughing. "Come on. I watched all three of you do your own downward spirals after you had women problems. I was there for you and didn't tell you what to do."

"That's true," Jace said.

"But we didn't carry on for three months, cause random destruction of property, and commit an assault," Alix pointed out.

"Also true," Jace added.

Rather than snapping at them like I wanted to, telling them that they didn't get it because they'd all found what they'd been looking for, I flipped them off. "I think, after a lifetime of being the guy who always does the right thing I've earned the right to a couple mistakes."

I didn't see them look at each other, but I felt it. I knew they were trying to figure out how far to push because I'd been on their side of things, needing to decide what to say and how to say it.

"You guys don't have to worry," I said, swiping Alix's drink. "Chester got me a PR rep."

"Seriously?" Erik said, his expression incredulous. "That's his solution for all of this?"

I glanced at him. "He trusts me to deal with my shit on my own. Paige's job is to fix my image."

There was a moment of silence, and then Jace asked, "Your PR rep's name is Paige?"

The tension in the air eased. "That it is," I said. "And she's hot. A pain in the ass, but what a fine ass."

As my friends laughed and started talking about their significant others, I let my thoughts turn to my hot PR rep and that fine ass of hers.

SEVEN
PAIGE

"He needs to be accessible," I said, dictating to my phone as I twisted my chair back and forth. My fingers worked a stress ball as I passed it back and forth between my hands. The repetitive movement was soothing, helping me stay focused on the task at hand.

Or as focused as I could be when my attention kept wanting to wander in inappropriate directions.

Like to the way his jeans had shown off strong, lean legs and a firm ass that made me want to sink my teeth–

"If we want people to forgive him for being human, he has to show them that he's human. No suits or tuxes. He needs to avoid the black-tie charity events where the attendees are all wealthy."

He definitely looked good in a tux. Something about the contrast between his tattoos and slightly scruffy rock star image, and the polished, debonair look just did it for me.

No. I needed to stop. Not just because he was a client, but because even if he wasn't, nothing would happen between us. I wasn't interested in being another notch on his bedpost. I had too much self-respect to act like I needed someone like him if I wanted to get off.

"During initial discussions, Mr. Union was unable to offer any suggestions about what could be done to improve his image. Recommendations to abstain from alcohol were met with silence and barely concealed hostility, so there's a possibility – probability – that Mr. Union's antics aren't yet over. We need to have a plan in place to deal with future instances."

I really hoped that wasn't going to be the case. I knew that, technically, it would be financially advantageous to have a client who repeatedly got into trouble and needed us to fix things. The bigger the project, the more billable hours. But I didn't want this thing with Reb to turn out that way. Which meant I needed to go beyond a surface fix and find out the reasons behind his behavior.

I continued my dictation, "Cursory investigation into Mr. Union's past revealed no known issues with alcohol or disorderly conduct, which begs the question...why now? What prompted a formerly almost-too-clean-for-a-rock-artist to suddenly go off the deep end?"

Just because he hadn't made a public spectacle of himself until recently didn't necessarily mean that something had happened in the past couple weeks. I'd seen several news stories from June that had talked about him breaking up with his girlfriend. His behavior hadn't been called into question back then since it had appeared to be a relatively harmless bit of brooding. Maybe the reports were mistaken. Brooding could have been a cover for drinking, even drugs. I'd heard rumors that some coke had even been found in his hotel room. His manager had been the one to hire us, and he'd said alcohol was Reb's drug of choice, but it wouldn't be the first time a manager hadn't known all of his client's dirty little secrets. And it definitely wouldn't have been the first time a manager had covered for one of his clients either.

I frowned as I squeezed the stress ball. Was Reb really the sort of man who'd be so broken up over a woman that he'd be drinking enough three months later to do what he'd done? Everything I'd observed about people in the entertainment industry, in general, told me that only a small percentage of them managed to have long-term relationships. Most of them went through romantic partners like they did clothes. The articles I'd read had said that Reb had been with his girlfriend for ten months. A lifetime for someone in his profession, but I still thought it seemed overly dramatic to still be so upset.

Unless he'd seen a future with her.

Was that even a possibility? I hadn't seen anything in the news about him ring shopping, gossip about wedding venues. I didn't remember any interviews where he or the girlfriend – Misty? Mitzi? – said anything about marriage, but that didn't necessarily mean anything. They could be one of those couples who didn't believe in institutionalized marriage.

I needed more insight before I could do anything, I reluctantly admitted to myself.

"Mr. Union has been relatively private about his personal life," I said into my phone. "Most media reports are based on speculations or interviews with people close to Mr. Union rather than direct conversations with him. To get real insight into his life, I'll have to talk directly to the sources of the articles. Or..." I paused, torn between anticipation and annoyance, "I'll have to speak to Mr. Union himself."

I glanced at the time. Nearly noon.

I stopped recording and set my stress ball down on the desk. I could track down people who knew Reb, ask them what they knew. They'd probably be able to fill in the blanks I needed.

But I didn't want to do that. I wanted to talk to him. Even though I tried to tell myself that it was because it was a simpler solution than going to several different sources, I knew a part of me wanted to see him again.

I stood and smoothed down my skirt. Physical attraction wasn't going to stop me from doing my job the best way possible. He was good-looking. So were a lot of men. I'd resisted the charms of better men than Reb Union.

I'd go to see him after lunch, ask him about the things I needed to know, and then I'd go straight back to the office and put together a strategy to improve his image quickly. Once he was back on top, I could move on to other clients and forget all about him.

The nagging voice in the back of my head piped up that it might be easier said than done.

IT WASN'T as hard to knock on his door the second time because I knew what to expect. More or less anyway.

"Back again?" Reb asked as he opened the door. "Come on in."

I followed him into the apartment, noting the empty bottles on the table in front of the couch. Unless he'd had friends over and hadn't cleaned up yet, he hadn't taken my 'advice' about not drinking.

"Sorry," he said, turning to face me. "I wasn't expecting company."

I gestured toward the table. "So these are all yours?"

He shrugged and shuffled his feet, thrusting a hand through his bronze hair. "Some friends stopped by last night."

I raised an eyebrow. Friends or not, he'd been drinking already this morning. "I came by to talk to you about a few things, but if I'm interrupting..."

"S'okay." The words weren't slurred, but they definitely weren't precise either. "You can stay. Want something to drink?"

I took a couple steps toward him, fixing my sternest expression on my face. "You need to take this seriously, Mr. Union."

"*Mr. Union?*" He snorted a laugh, the sound almost enough to startle a smile out of me.

That was definitely not the sort of laugh I expected from someone like him. With a mother who was a visible member of New York high society, I'd seen numerous pictures of him schmoozing with the cream of the crop. People who weren't just rich, but old money. Politicians and philanthropists. The kind of people who practiced their smiles and laughs in front of a mirror so they'd be absolutely perfect. Not too big or loud, not too small or soft.

Definitely not the kind of people who snorted.

Still, I couldn't let his response go unanswered. "Do you find this amusing?"

He closed the distance between us, and under the smell of whiskey, I caught a whiff of soap. At least he'd taken a shower since I'd seen him last.

"Nothing about this is amusing, Miss Ryce." He frowned, his gaze dropping to my mouth before coming back up to meet my eyes. "Is it Mrs. or Miss? I don't see a ring, but that doesn't always mean single."

I fought the urge to cross my arms, knowing that with him looming over me, it would come across as defensive rather than annoyed. "Let's stick to the matter at hand, Mr. Union."

"Reb," he corrected. "I get enough 'Mr. Union' from brown-nosers and ass-kissers."

"We need to maintain professional boundaries," I argued. "I'm not here to be your friend."

"That's good," he said, his voice deepened, roughened. "Because I have enough friends."

I could feel a flush creeping up my neck, and I clenched my hands into fists. "Mr—"

"You're an employee, right?" he asked, taking a step in my direction. "I mean, technically, I hired you, right?"

Reluctantly, I nodded. I wasn't sure I liked where this was heading.

"Then I'm your boss." He grinned, his eyes lighting up. "And I'm telling you to call me Reb."

In the back of my mind, I could hear my mother telling me to pick my battles. She told me more than once that was how she'd kept a balance when it came to discipline. Treating him like a child seemed like the best way to go.

"All right...Reb." I spoke through gritted teeth, but it was enough to satisfy him.

"Thank you. Now, tell me, *Paige*," his voice slid across my name like a caress, "is there a Mr. Ryce?"

I shook my head. This was a bad idea. I was supposed to be getting background information on him, not the other way around. How had I lost control of the situation so quickly?

"Is there someone gunning for the position?"

"No," I said, hating the breathless way the word came out. "I'm single. Now that we got that out of the way, can we—"

My sentence was cut off as Reb wrapped a hand around the back of my neck and pulled me to him, our mouths crashing together in an explosive kiss.

EIGHT
PAIGE

For the first time in my life, my mind failed me. I couldn't think about anything other than the heat of his mouth on mine, the taste of expensive whiskey when he slid his tongue across mine, the feel of his strong fingers on my neck.

I only had a few kisses to compare this one to, but I had a feeling that it wouldn't have mattered if I'd had a thousand kisses before. Nothing else would feel like this. Like every cell in my body was suddenly awake in a way it'd never been before. Awake, and aware of this new humming electricity that flowed between the two of us.

Almost involuntarily, my arms went up and around his neck, his hair soft against my fingers. He made a sound in the back of his throat, a hungry, desperate sound, and then his free hand gripped my hip. When his teeth grazed my bottom lip, the shock of it jarred me back to my senses, and I took a step back.

My breath was ragged, and as I looked at Reb, I could see that he was just as affected as I was. That didn't make me feel any better though. If anything, I felt worse. My first client and I'd kissed him...no, *he'd* kissed *me*.

"I'm flattered, Mr. Union."

His entire body went stiff, his expression hardening.

"But I'm here as your PR rep, nothing else. I shouldn't have let...I mean, that shouldn't have happened."

He nodded and turned away. "Of course not. Sorry about that. Misread the situation."

"It's all right," I conceded, but something about the slump of his shoulders told me that something was off. This wasn't just some rejected kiss to him, though I wasn't arrogant enough to think that this was because of me specifically.

"Don't worry about it." He dropped onto the couch and picked up the only bottle that still contained some liquid. "It's not the first time I've been rejected by a woman for what I wanted."

I'd been considering walking away and leaving him to whatever pity-party he'd been throwing for himself, but I didn't hear just bitterness in his voice. There was sadness there too...and self-loathing.

No matter how much I told myself that it wasn't my job to get personally involved, I couldn't bring myself to walk away.

"What do you mean? Rejected for what you wanted?"

He drained the last of the whiskey and tossed the bottle to the other end of the couch. "Shouldn't you be going? Running away from the deviant after your precious virtue."

I flushed and told myself that he was drunk, rambling, probably didn't know what he was saying. Hell, he probably wouldn't even remember any of this tomorrow.

But this wasn't about a kiss, and to do my job, I needed to know what was going on. That was why I'd come here, after all.

I walked over to the couch and sat on the arm. It was far enough away from him that we weren't touching, but close enough that he'd feel more like he was talking to a friend than someone grilling him.

"What's going on?" When he didn't answer, I added, "I can't help you if you don't talk to me."

"Why would you want to help me?" he asked, looking up at me. His eyes were dark and open. Sad. "You didn't want me kissing you, and I thought it was a good kiss. Thought you wanted me to kiss you, but I was wrong. Not the first time I didn't know what a woman wanted. I used to think I did."

"You're not making any sense," I said. What he was saying should have put me off. All of it sounded like the kind of shit an egotistical little prick would say to get a woman in bed.

But something told me that wasn't what he was doing right now.

"You might as well know. Nobody else does, but at least you'll know, and you can get out while you can. Flee the sinking ship." He made a disgusted sound and smacked the couch with the flat of his hand.

He really needed to quit drinking. This would do worse things for his reputation than trashing a hotel room or punching someone. Fans could handle their rock stars behaving like assholes, but this was the wrong side of vulnerable.

"I'm guessing you did your homework because Chester would have only hired the best, so you know about the break-up." He glanced at me, and I nodded but didn't say anything. He continued anyway, "She wasn't living with me, Mitzi, I mean, but she stayed at my place when we were in New York. She had problems, and I knew it, but she didn't want to talk about them, so I didn't."

He picked at a thread on the couch, and I wondered if he felt more like he was talking to himself rather than me.

"I came in one day and found her in bed with a couple roadies. She was strung out and didn't even blink when she saw me. She just kept fucking them and told me that it was all my fault. That if I hadn't made her do..." His voice trailed off, and he raised his head. "I've *never* forced a woman to do anything. You have to believe me."

Even if my gut hadn't been telling me that he wouldn't do that, I could hear the desperation in his voice, and it wasn't because he wanted me to believe him. He wanted to believe it himself.

"I believe you," I said gently.

He'd been drunk when he kissed me, but he still let me go when I'd taken a step back. If he was the sort of guy who would force what he wanted on someone, that would've been a perfect opportunity to do it. But he hadn't.

Maybe he wasn't as bad as I'd originally thought.

"You're pretty," he mumbled as his head dropped forward, chin on his chest.

I sighed. "Okay, you're going to get a crick in your neck if you sleep like that."

I stood up and then reached down to get a firm hold under his arm. He was bigger than me, but I was stronger than I looked. It took some maneuvering, but I managed to get him to his feet. He kept muttering random things under his breath, but I didn't bother trying to figure out what he was saying. I was pretty sure I'd figured out the incident that had triggered his change in behavior. Now, I just had to get him sobered up and then we could get started on rehabbing his career.

NINE
REB

Something was off.

The pounding in my head was familiar and expected. So was the bed. Except I wasn't supposed to be in this bed. Why was I here instead of at a hotel?

Oh. Right. Because I'd done some stupid shit and coming back here had been my only option. Well, the lesser of all the evils offered. No way in hell would I stay with my mom, or with my friends.

So, I'd come home. As my brain sluggishly woke, I realized that I still didn't know why I was in my bed. I'd slept on the couch before because I hadn't wanted to be in here.

Before I could try to sort things out any further, my body let me know that I'd been out for a long time. It was probably a miracle I hadn't pissed the bed. Passing out drunk often didn't guarantee the ability to wake up for the call of nature.

I groaned as I climbed out of bed, my joints stiff and

aching. Everything of mine ached, actually. I limped into my bathroom, my hands keeping me from stumbling into something I couldn't see in the dim light. I could have turned on the lights, but I had a feeling that might make me throw up, and cleaning up puke was not what I needed right now.

I breathed a sigh of relief as I emptied my bladder. Tempted as I was to go straight for my liquor cabinet, I was already in the bathroom, so a shower was probably a good idea. After everything that'd happened, I needed to at least put forth an effort, or all my years of hard work were going to burn right in front of me.

I drank a glass of water as I waited a few seconds for the water to heat up. Maybe after I'd had some of the expensive scotch I'd gotten from someone, I'd call Chester and find out if he'd gotten any feedback from the PR firm. Paige hadn't liked me much, which made me wonder if she was going to request a change. I hoped she didn't, and it wasn't only because I thought she was hot.

She hadn't been impressed by me. In fact, I'd gotten the impression that she really didn't care what I thought about her beyond her ability to do her job. She'd held her own with me, both yesterday when we first met and then earlier today…

Shit.

She'd come back over.

I leaned out of the shower to check the clock on the bathroom wall. Six o'clock. Was that morning or evening? The last thing I remembered was talking to Paige. It had been afternoon. Maybe. But I didn't feel like I'd slept for only a few hours.

My alcohol-soaked brain struggled to put the pieces together, but it took until I was toweling off before I was able to process that it had to be six in the morning. I'd slept for more than twelve hours. My stomach growled, as if it had needed the acknowledgment of time to be allowed to announce how long it had been since I'd eaten.

I wrapped my towel around my waist and started toward the kitchen. Breakfast first. *Then* I'd call Chester and have him send Paige a nice fruit basket or something in case I said something rude yesterday. I didn't think so, but it never hurt to be cautious.

I was halfway down the hall when something new caught my attention. I smelled food. Specifically, bacon and coffee. Someone was here, but considering they were cooking, I felt safe in assuming they weren't here to hurt me. My stomach rumbled again, and I walked faster. I'd never seen Chester cook, so I doubted I'd find him waiting for me, which meant it was most likely my mother. At the moment, I was prepared to happily trade a lecture for some breakfast.

The person standing at the stove, however, wasn't my mother. I'd only met her twice, but I had no problem recognizing Paige, even from the back.

"Did you stay the whole night?"

She jumped, then turned, the startled expression on her face shifting to something else for a moment before disappearing behind a mask of indifference. If I hadn't known better, I would've said she was checking me out... because I was wearing only a towel. Shit.

"Sorry," I apologized. "I forgot I wasn't wearing–"

"You've been asleep for more than a day," she interrupted, the look on her face telling me that she wasn't going to acknowledge my lack of clothes. "It's Thursday evening."

I shook my head. "That's not possible. I would've had to get up."

She turned back to the stove. "You did," she said. "Sort of."

"What does that mean?"

She hesitated, and I had a feeling I wasn't going to like what she had to say.

"What do you remember from yesterday?"

I ran a hand through my hair, sending droplets of water raining down on my shoulders. "Um, not a lot. My friends came over...no, wait, that was Tuesday. Yesterday. Right, Wednesday. I remember you being here. We talked. It's all really fuzzy."

"That's all?"

Shit. "Did I do something? If I offended you, I'm sorry–"

"No," she said sharply. "We talked. I put you into the closest bed I could find."

"That's a guest room," I interrupted with a frown. "Did I move into my room at some point?"

"Yes. Sometime late last night, you..." Her voice trailed off and even with her back to me, I could see that the tips of her ears were red, but I didn't think it was because of me and the towel this time. "I put the bed linens in the washer, along with your clothes. Once I cleaned you up and put you in your bed, I called a cleaning company. They'll come do a deep clean on the mattress whenever you want."

Heat rushed to my face. "I'm sorry about that. I should've known better than to finish vodka on an empty stomach. I can usually hold my liquor better."

She turned around but refused to look at me as she held out a plate. "Yeah, well, no one can hold that much liquid that long."

I took the plate, set it on the table, and then froze as I realized what she'd said could have meant something completely different than my original thought. I closed my eyes. "Please tell me that I didn't piss the bed." She didn't say anything, and that just made it worse. "Please tell me that I didn't piss the bed like some kid and you had to clean up after me."

"Don't worry." Her voice was dry. "I'm billing you for everything."

I hung my head and wished this was a dream. "And here I thought I'd already hit rock bottom."

I felt a hand on my arm, and I jerked my head up, my eyes meeting hers. There was a hint of humor in those blue-green irises. "Don't worry. Your confidentiality agreement with my company completely guarantees my silence."

"Yeah, that doesn't really make me feel any better."

She took a step back, the humor falling away. "Let's get some coffee and food in you, then we can talk."

I didn't like the sound of that. The talking. The other stuff actually sounded pretty good.

After I'd gone back to my room to put on pants – and a shirt – I returned to the kitchen and took a seat at the waiting plate. I took a few bites of bacon, and then asked, "Did I do anything else I need to apologize for?"

She didn't answer, which made me think there was something she didn't want to tell me, and considering what she'd already told me, I couldn't imagine what would possibly be–

Her hair was like silk against the back of my hand, her skin almost as soft. My thumb found the hollow behind her ear as my fingers curled around her neck and pulled her toward me. This was a bad idea, but I had to know what she tasted like, what her lips felt like. My mouth came down on hers, and it was like nothing I'd felt before. Heat and electricity, all of it narrowed down to a single point of contact. And then she had her hands in my hair, her body pressing against mine. Fuck, those curves...

My hand tightened around my coffee mug. I wanted to believe that I was remembering a dream, but my body told me it'd really happened. It remembered better than my head what it had felt like to have her in my arms.

"Paige, I am so sorry. I was out of–"

"The drinking needs to stop," she said briskly, acting as if she hadn't heard what I'd been trying to say. "Not just cut back, but actually stop. No more alcohol until I say it's okay."

That got my attention. Not because of the drinking, but because she thought she could actually give me an order. Aside from my mother, no one told me what to do. It actually made me smile.

I stood up and picked up my now-empty plate. "What if I don't want to stop?" I turned toward her, actually curious to hear her answer.

Her eyes narrowed as she closed the distance between us. Even though I was dressed, she kept her eyes on mine. She was as close as she'd been before, when I'd kissed her, but I had a feeling that if I tried that now, she'd probably slap me. Or bite me.

That last thought shouldn't have sent blood rushing straight to my cock.

"I was hired to do a job, Mr. Union." She put her hands on her hips. "*This* is how the job gets done. *This* is how I save your image."

Her eyes were sparking, showing me that I hadn't imagined her fire. I wanted to reach out and touch her, see how she'd respond. She was strong, stubborn, independent...all of the things that should have turned me off as a Dom. Even with vanilla sex, I needed the control, the challenge.

Paige was definitely a challenge.

"If you're not willing to do what I ask, then maybe we need to find someone else to take my place."

Hell no. This was just getting interesting.

"Maybe I just need the right incentive," I suggested. I gave her a slow, thorough look, letting myself see all the things my subconscious had registered before.

Damn.

"What do you say, Paige? I do what you ask, and I get rewarded?"

TEN
PAIGE

"That's not how this works, Mr. Union. I think it'd be best for everyone if I spoke to my boss and had someone new take over."

That was what I should have said. I'd gone above and beyond the call of duty with him. I'd spent more than a day taking care of him, and that was so far out of my job description that I could make a case to Sybil to drop him completely as a client. I had a degree in public relations, not babysitting or housekeeping. No offense meant to anyone who worked in either of those fields. I respected the hard work it took to take care of kids and homes. But this wasn't my home, and Reb was definitely *not* a kid.

I'd seen that for myself. Not that I'd doubted his masculinity before, but now I had visual proof burned into my mind.

He'd been half-conscious when I'd stripped off his clothes and cleaned him up. Not awake enough to have a coherent conversation, but enough that I wasn't trying to move him around on my own. I told myself over and over that it was no different than helping my mom bathe my grandfather after his stroke, but...no, it wasn't the same at all.

And I couldn't get the memory of those amazingly defined muscles and that long, thick–

Dammit.

This wasn't the time or the place for me to be ogling a guy, and it was never the time or place for me to ogle a client. I wasn't immune to the fact that Reb was gorgeous, but that wasn't the point. Nothing was going to happen between us. Nothing *could* happen between us.

And I preferred it that way.

Which meant I needed to take back control of the situation before it got any further away from me than it already was.

"If you have anything planned for Saturday, cancel it." The expression on Reb's face told me the direction of his thoughts, and I mentally cursed myself for not being more put off by it. My irritation at myself came out in my next statement. "You're doing charity work."

"I am?" He didn't seem annoyed, but rather amused.

"You are." I did my best to keep from returning his smile. The fact that I was torn between wanting to kick him or kiss him didn't make his grin any less infectious. I took a step back to put some distance between us, but it didn't stop me from being able to feel the tension between us, the very thing I'd felt before we kissed. That couldn't happen again.

No matter how much my mouth still burned from just the memory.

"That's your brilliant PR plan? Have me do a little charity work, and all will be forgotten?" He shook his head. "I thought you were smarter than that."

My temper flared, and I crowded into his space, glaring up at him. "Just because you're paying–"

Before I finished the sentence, I saw the corner of his mouth twitch and realized he'd been intentionally goading me.

Asshole.

"Look," I snapped. "This isn't going to be some 'one and done' thing. The shit may not have hit the fan until recently, but you've been spiraling for months, and everyone knows it. It's going to take more than one Saturday picking up litter if you want to move beyond 'paid your debt to society' and on to salvaging your image as a good guy."

"You think I'm a good guy?"

I sighed. He wasn't going to make this easy for me. "Fine. You do what I tell you to do, and do it well. In return, I'll make sure you get something for your troubles."

He grinned. "Then I put myself in your hands."

I tried to think of the most bland, platonic way to take that statement. "I'll send you a text with the time and place tomorrow."

Then, before he could see me flustered, I excused

myself and left. I needed to get home anyway. I needed to have a good meal, and a good night's sleep, especially since I'd be working over the weekend. I told Reb the truth when I said the company would be billing for the time I'd spent, but a little voice at the back of my head wondered if I'd have stayed even if that hadn't been possible.

By the time I arrived home, all of my frustration from the past week had coiled into a tight ball in the middle of my stomach. Going into public relations, I'd known that I'd be asked to work with people I disliked. While not all clients were people in trouble looking to smooth things over, there were enough that I knew, sooner or later, there'd be someone I found distasteful.

Except, if I was honest with myself, I didn't actually dislike Reb. He got under my skin in a way that no one else had been able to, and I didn't like that, but if I'd met Reb under different circumstances, we might have gotten along. I still wouldn't have dated him, of course, because I was sticking to my life-long resolution to avoid romantic entanglements with people in his line of work.

I reheated some take-out and wrote myself a note to pick up some groceries on my way home from work tomorrow. My supplies were looking a bit sparse. I didn't have the time to cook myself dinner every night, but I tried to get at least a couple home-cooked meals a week.

I ate standing up, tidying up the kitchen as I went. I moved on automatic pilot, making mental lists of all the things I needed to do tomorrow to get things set up for Saturday. I had a couple ideas of places where Reb could do community service, so that was the first thing to get settled. Once I did that, I could leak information to the media. I didn't want to give a direct invitation to news outlets, even though most of them would guess a PR firm of some kind was involved. That's just how things worked, especially when the client was in the entertainment industry.

One of the interns at the firm had an uncle who owned a huge construction company that often worked with Habitat for Humanity. I'd check there first to see if they had any projects this weekend that Reb could work on. The press would have a field day with pictures of him lifting things, hammering…sweating…

"Dammit," I muttered the curse as I put away the last of the dishes, but I couldn't chase away the images that came up, one after the other.

Reb wiping his face off with the bottom of his shirt, showing off that flat, tight stomach, and the trail of golden brown hair that disappeared under the waistband of his pants. Jeans that hung low enough on his hips that I could see those amazing v-grooves. Pulling his shirt over his head to reveal rippling muscles and tattoos I wanted to trace with my tongue…

Fuck.

I needed a shower. A cold shower. Now.

But when I went into the bathroom, I changed my mind. I needed to get rid of this tension, and it was getting late. I could combine cleaning up with getting some relief, and maybe that would even get Reb out of my head. I had to focus on correcting his image, not that amazing body of his.

As I washed, I tried to pull up one of the fantasies that had worked for me in the past. A hot model I'd seen on a billboard. A favorite character on a television show. A completely imagined man who knew exactly what to do with my body.

But every single one of them morphed into Reb, that smirk on his face and heat in his eyes. So I gave up and closed my eyes, letting my imagination wander even as my hands did the same.

I ran one hand over my breasts, fingers teasing my nipples as I imagined the rough callouses on his fingers scraping over my skin. His lips moving down my throat, teeth nipping at me until I knew he'd left little marks. My free hand went between my legs, moving over the thin curls that covered me until my fingers reached my clit. I circled the already throbbing bundle of nerves, thinking about how he'd touch me there. Rough, hard passes until his mouth soothed me. Just the right amount of suction.

It was the thought of looking down and seeing Reb's head between my legs, tongue and fingers driving me toward orgasm that undid me. The muscles in my body tensed as a small cry escaped me.

Even as the release eased the tension in my body, I couldn't help but think that I'd made a mistake.

ELEVEN
REB

What the hell had I been thinking? She worked for me – sort of – and I'd been teasing her. Flirting with her. It hadn't really been a conscious decision on my part, but that was no excuse. I'd been completely unprofessional.

I snorted a laugh. I'd been drunk pretty much from moment one with her. She'd put me to bed, cleaned me up when I pissed myself, then put me to bed again.

I'd *kissed* her, for fuck's sake. My flirting was low on the list of unprofessional things I'd done with her, and it didn't even register on the list of stupid shit I'd done lately.

Hell, it hadn't even really been flirting.

No, that was a lie. I might not have *said* anything overtly sexual, but I'd *meant* it. She was beautiful, the sort of woman that men would stare at as she walked by. That women would hate on sight alone. That anyone remotely attracted to women would fantasize about.

It was more than physical with her though.

When it came to women who looked like her, some honestly didn't know they were beautiful, some pretended not to know, and some used their beauty like a weapon. Paige was one of the rarest kind though. The kind of woman who understood her physical appeal, but made certain it wasn't the most important thing about her.

She was smart, clever, the kind of quick wit that startled and surprised. Hell, it'd gotten a laugh out of me more than once. And she had a steel backbone, more guts than most people, and I wanted to know what it would take to make her submit...

"Knock it off." I said the words out loud because I thought it'd make a difference, but it didn't. I just kept on thinking about Paige, and the way those eyes of hers had flashed when she'd gotten in my face.

What color would they turn when she was aroused, I wondered. Something like the ocean, I imagined. Not like the pure blue coasts in the Caribbean, but rather something deeper, darker.

Then there was that blush. Her skin was so fair that she couldn't hide it, and I wanted to know what it was like to see it spread over her entire body. That wasn't the only color I was interested seeing on her either. Another form of red and pink appealed to me. My handprint on her ass. Stripes from a flogger and crop.

Now that I'd let my mind go there, I didn't want to stop imagining. If I was going to stop drinking, I needed something else to take my mind off of things and thinking about how Paige would reward me this weekend would definitely do the trick.

I sat down on the couch and leaned my head back, closing my eyes. I could picture her immediately. Every line and curve of her face. I shouldn't have been able to see her so clearly, but there she was.

And I could just imagine what it would be like to have her smile at me as she knelt in front of me.

"Hands behind your back," I ordered.

She immediately obeyed, the position pushing her ample breasts out even more. Her nipples, a pale, delicate rose color, were pinched between a set of clamps, but no discomfort showed on her face. All I could see was a desire to please. To please me.

"Open your mouth."

She parted her lips, and I reached out to brush my thumb across her bottom lip. I'd kissed her, bitten the soft, plump flesh, but now I wanted her lips wrapped around my cock.

I gripped my shaft in one hand and buried my other in her hair. "Look at me."

I waited until our eyes met and then slid my cock into her mouth. I groaned as the velvet heat enveloped me. It didn't matter how many times she did this, it was always like heaven.

She let me guide her head, offering no resistance as I made her take me deeper and deeper. Her breathing was harsh, mingling with the slick, wet sound of her mouth on me.

"Do you want me to come in your mouth?" I asked, my voice tight. *"Or on your face?"*

I cursed as I fisted my cock faster, the pressure inside me building with each stroke.

"You choose, my Paige," I said as I pulled back far enough for my dick to slide free. *"Where do you want me to come?"* I asked again. *"Mouth? Face?"* Each suggestion made a pulse of lust go through me. *"Tits?"*

Her breathing hitched. "Wherever you want, Sir."

I shook my head. "No, Paige, I want you to choose. Where do you want me to come?"

The words were barely a whisper. "Inside me, Sir."

"Say that again," I growled.

She squared her shoulders and spoke louder. "I want you to come in my pussy, Sir."

"Fuck!" The word tore out of me as I climaxed, spurting over my fist and onto my shirt. I was a mess, but the pressure inside me was gone. For the first time in months, my head was clear.

Well, *that* was unexpected.

TWELVE

PAIGE

Considering the guilt that had swept over me after I'd gotten off while fantasizing about Reb, it was probably a good thing that Habitat for Humanity didn't have anything going on at the moment. I wasn't sure I could take an entire morning of watching Reb doing construction work and be able to control myself.

Fortunately, I'd gotten ahold of Candra Hammel, a college classmate of mine who now ran a community program where kids could go both after school and on the weekends. While, most of the time, they had the usual games and such, sometimes they brought in people to offer specialized classes or workshops. Today, they were getting rock star Reb Union to teach music to the kids.

I just hoped I'd made the right call. If he showed up drunk or behaved like an ass, I'd be lucky to not get fired. Reb wasn't the only one putting things on the line today.

"Candra." I smiled at the woman standing by the front door. She looked just as polished and professional as ever. "It's good to see you again."

"You too," she said as she gave me a hug. "It looks like all that hard work you put in is paying off. Representing Reb Union." She let out a low whistle, her turquoise eyes sparkling. "I know a lot of women who'd give their right arm to get that close to him."

I didn't have to ask if she was one of them. Candra had been an out and proud lesbian since well before I knew her. She'd appreciate Reb's beauty the same way I appreciated hers, but it wouldn't be an issue. That wasn't the main reason I'd gone to her, but it was definitely a bonus.

"He's my first client," I admitted. "The first one I have by myself, anyway. I have to get it right."

Candra nodded. "At least you've got a good guy to work with."

"You know him?" I was pleased to hear that I didn't sound as surprised as I actually was. I didn't want her getting the wrong idea, because I wasn't jealous. He wasn't her type. And even if he was, it wouldn't have mattered because he wasn't *my* type.

"Only by reputation. He has a good one." She frowned, and her gaze drifted away from mine. "At least he did until recently. His break-up appeared to have really hit him hard. It's good that she's gone though. Mitzi was clearly using him."

I stared at her. Candra hadn't been as much of a

workaholic as me, but she'd always been focused. The attention to the entertainment industry was new.

She laughed at the expression on my face. "My girlfriend works at *Entertainment Weekly*."

"So, you know that I–"

"Leaked that Reb would be here today?" She finished. "I figured that'd be the case even before I got Lena's message."

"I don't want you to think I'm using the program. I think it's amazing what you do for these kids."

She smiled. "I know. It's okay. Generally, when celebrities come to something like this, it's for publicity reasons, and I'd much rather have someone like Reb come in and actually do something other than write a check."

"I'll make sure he behaves himself," I promised. I wasn't sure how I was going to manage that, but I'd think of something. My ears grew hot as I remembered telling him that I'd make sure he 'got something' out of this. I'd come up with something appropriately professional. No way in hell would I give in to the thoughts I knew had accompanied his request for a 'reward.' I didn't want that.

"Speak of the devil," Candra said, looking past me.

I didn't need to turn to know he was coming right for us. I could feel him staring and prayed that Candra didn't read anything into it. The last thing Reb needed was rumors that something was going on between him and his PR rep. I didn't even want to think what it would do to my reputation.

"I've got to get inside," Candra said. "Two of my usual volunteers called in sick this morning. The kids that get here this early always have far too much energy, and if I don't give them something constructive to do, I'll end up cleaning paint off my ceiling."

The expression on her face said that she hadn't pulled something that specific out of nowhere. I really hoped Reb was up to this. Maybe scheduling things without talking them through with him wasn't such a good idea. I'd figured making the decisions on my own would keep him from arguing about them. The longer this dragged out, the harder it was going to be to stop the momentum. He needed to do something as soon as possible to show that he was trying to change his image.

Reb stopped next to me as Candra hurried off. "Did I do something to offend her?" he asked.

I shook my head as I turned toward him. "She's a bit understaffed this morning." I glanced down to see that he'd brought a guitar with him like I'd asked. "Thanks for bringing that."

"It's been a long time since I've played an acoustic guitar with nothing else backing me up."

I gave him a sharp look, but he wasn't complaining like I'd thought. He almost looked excited by the idea. "The kids who come here are pretty much all from this neighborhood. Mostly good families, but ones that don't have the money or time to send their kids to lessons. It's not gangs or drugs that are the biggest danger here, but rather the inability to do anything else."

He looked around, a thoughtful expression on his face.

"Some will be talented enough to become electricians or mechanics, and they'll do well. They'll be the success stories. But the kids who might've become doctors, lawyers, teachers, counselors – the sort of occupations that need a college degree – they'll find themselves working in stores or on construction crews. They'll never have the chance to reach their full potential. Maybe some will be able to get into college, get some small scholarships, but they won't be able to afford to go."

I remembered when I first realized what it meant that I was going to college. Mom had always made it clear to me that I either had to learn a trade or pursue a degree. Both were equally valuable, but I was expected to excel in whatever path I chose to pursue.

I had pushed myself academically, even doubling up on credits so I could graduate a year early. I'd earned several scholarships, but if it hadn't been for my mother's determination that I get to do what I wanted, I wouldn't have made it. For as long as I could remember, she'd worked two jobs, gone without so many things, all so she could make sure I didn't need to work. It was thanks to her I'd been able to accept an unpaid internship my senior year, and I'd felt like all the hard work had paid off when I'd gotten hired as a paid employee.

Any time I'd gotten tired and considered quitting, I'd think about my mom and how, some nights, she'd fallen asleep on the couch, half-way through her dinner.

"Paige?"

I gave myself a mental shake and smiled at Reb. I hadn't asked him if working with kids was okay, and now I wondered if he'd even be able to relate or if I'd set us up to fail.

"Candra wants you to play a couple songs, then work on teaching the kids about music. Once we see how things go, she'll probably have you repeat things every few hours so kids who come in later will get the same chance."

"All right," he agreed. "Let's get started."

I watched him as he walked toward the double doors. He didn't look drunk, despite being a little rough around the edges. I hoped that meant he was going to listen to me when I told him what to do. He didn't give me the impression that he was a man who was accustomed to taking orders, much less obeying them. In fact, something about the way he carried himself made me think that not many people bossed him around, not without repercussions of some kind.

Something low in me throbbed at the thoughts of rewards and punishment, but I didn't let it linger. We had work to do.

Any doubts I had about how he'd do with kids vanished the moment we stepped inside the community center.

"Holy shit!" A boy who looked to be about ten or so shouted as soon as he saw Reb. "That's Reb Union! He's a total badass!"

"Tyler!" Candra scolded him. "What have we said about language?"

He gave her the sort of charming grin that I bet he used on most authority figures to get away with things. "That the study of the English language is fucking important?"

"Tyler!" She was trying to stay firm, but I could tell she was trying not to laugh. "Mind your manners."

He bounced up and down on his toes, but stayed where he was, and didn't shout again.

"Kids," Candra addressed the whole group. "Mr. Union is our special guest today. He's going to be playing some songs for you, and then he's going to teach you a bit about music." She gave Tyler a stern look. "Which means, I expect all of you to be on your best behavior. Is that understood?"

"Yes, Ms. Hammel," the whole group chorused.

Candra turned to Reb. "Think you can take it from here?"

He swallowed hard, and I wondered if anyone else could tell that he was nervous. "I can. Thank you."

He smiled and led the kids over to a place at the other end of the building where a stage was set up. He sat down, taking out his guitar as the kids pulled chairs into a half-circle. I leaned back against the wall to watch.

Because I needed to make sure this worked.

Not because I wanted to watch him.

"All right," he said as he settled his guitar on his lap. "I'm guessing at least one of you knows some of my music. Do I have a request?"

"'Under the Waves,'" Tyler immediately spoke up. "That's my favorite song."

Reb nodded, plucking at a few strings. "That's one of my favorites too." His gaze flicked to me. "One of the first songs I ever wrote but fits my life now more than ever."

I ignored the warmth that spread through me at his look. It didn't mean anything.

Still, as he began to sing, I couldn't help but think about what it would be like to have someone like him singing to me. The lyrics of the song weren't romantic, but I still felt them. He meant every word, and that had nothing to do with trying to look professional.

"He's amazing."

I glanced over at Candra as she came to stand next to me. I didn't want to agree with her, but there was no way around it. She was right.

"The kids seem to like him," I said, hating myself for how non-committal it sounded.

"They do."

Reb finished up the song, and another kid piped up with a suggestion. They came, one right after the other, and he kept playing. He didn't complain, not even when one quiet looking girl shyly requested a song that was definitely *not* one of Reb's. Instead, he gave the kids a silly grin and began playing the cute, bouncy pop song.

After a couple hours, Candra pushed herself off the wall and interrupted, "Who's ready for their mid-morning snack?"

A chorus of cheers answered the question. Three kids hung back as the others rushed to the window where fruit and bottled water waited. One was Tyler, the boy who'd been scolded for his language, and he was hanging on Reb's every word. Another was the girl who'd asked for the pop song, and she looked like she was torn between wanting to talk to him and wanting to disappear. The third was a small, skinny boy who was trying to hide behind Tyler.

Curious to see how Reb would handle his little admirers, I waited and watched.

"Are you going to teach us how to play the guitar?" Tyler asked. "I'd be awesome."

"I bet you would," Reb said. He clapped a hand on Tyler's shoulder, then looked at the other two. "Hi."

The girl's cheeks flushed, and she ducked her head. "Hi."

"She's Mags," Tyler said. He smacked the other boy on the shoulder. "He's Larry."

"Nice to meet you."

Had he seriously just said *nice to meet you* to three kids who hadn't quite hit puberty? And now he was talking to them like he was their friend. Joking with them. Asking them questions about school and the things they liked to do. He told Larry to be proud of his photographic memory. Told Mags that she should just be herself. He sat with the kids as they ate their snacks and there wasn't a single trace of insincerity in anything he said.

Was it possible that *this* was who Reb really was? That he was a decent guy who loved kids? That the alcohol and bad decision making was a fluke?

No. I made myself look away, ignore what I was seeing. I couldn't afford to think that he was different. One morning spent with kids didn't make him a good guy.

I needed to remember that, and everything would be fine.

THIRTEEN
REB

I hadn't been dreading the community service itself – being sober again wasn't that great – but I hadn't expected to enjoy myself. I'd been looking forward to seeing Paige, even though I knew she was off limits, but when I walked into that community center and Tyler had yelled my name...I hadn't felt anything like that in a long time.

As I followed Tyler, Mags, and Larry over to where the rest of the kids were sitting, I realized that I was having fun. I'd loved performing unplugged, singing songs as the kids called them out. Hell, I'd even liked singing that pop song because it'd made Mags smile.

"So, how many of you think you might like to learn how to read and write music?" I asked.

Hands shot up, and I immediately started thinking of all the ways to best teach them how to read music. I'd never thought of myself as a teacher, but in that moment, I could see it. Showing the kids how to love music the way I did.

"Do you write all your own songs?" Tyler asked.

I nodded. "I do."

"Not all musicians do though, right?" Larry asked.

"Right," I said. "Sometimes, people are good at playing instruments or singing, and sometimes they're good at writing music and lyrics, but not always both."

"But you do both," Mags said.

I nodded again. "I do."

I didn't tell them that it'd been a while since I'd written anything. That the songs I'd sung this morning had been written years and months before. In my opinion, the quality had been going downhill too. The studio had been threatening to send in writers for me, to create an album that would take the charts by storm. Only the fact that I'd had it put into my contract that I had veto power on album content had kept them from doing it. If things were going to suck, I'd own it.

It was one of the reasons Chester had been on my ass. Fucking up my image would've been bad enough if I'd had a new album out or one coming out, but that could've been spun positively. The fact that they had to keep asking me when I was going to get into the studio and finally record something meant they hadn't been feeling very friendly toward me when the shit hit the fan.

But that was why I had Paige. She was going to fix all of that.

I forced my mind off of Paige as Candra announced it was time to move into the teaching music part of the morning. It was funny. I'd spent so much time drinking over the past few months because I wanted to forget, to get out of my head, and I hadn't been able to turn to music like I had in the past. Then I met Paige, and she became another thing I couldn't get out of my head, no matter how hard I tried.

Until I came here, stone cold sober for the first time since the beginning of summer, and found that I could focus on the music again. Playing it, at least. I still couldn't find it in me to focus on writing it, but I'd take what I could get.

"ALL RIGHT, LISTEN UP!"

Paige's friend, Candra, clapped her hands and waited until everyone's attention was on her.

"That's all for our special guest today." She held up her hands when several of the kids protested. "Please make sure to thank him for spending time with us, and then it's time for team sports."

We were done already? I looked at the clock and was surprised to see that it was nearly three in the afternoon. How had the time flown by so fast?

I didn't have a chance to think about it too much, however, because the kids were all coming over to say their goodbyes. Unsurprisingly, Tyler, Mags, and Larry all hung back, waiting until the others cleared out before they approached.

"Do you really have to go?" Tyler asked. "You're the first cool person we've ever had here."

The mutinous look on his face reminded me of my niece, Josie, when my sister would tell her she couldn't do something. Annette always blamed me for that.

"I think Ms. Hammel has some things planned for you guys to do now," I said.

"Team sports." Larry made a face. "No one ever wants us on their team, so we always play together."

"And we always lose," Mags added.

I glanced up to see Paige coming toward me, but as much as I wanted to try and get some alone time with her, I wanted to see these kids smile more. "How about if I play on your team?"

Their faces lit up.

"For real?" Mags asked, grabbing my hand.

I nodded. "For real." I smiled as they cheered. "So, what are we playing?"

"Soccer," Tyler said. "Come on!"

I followed the kids over to the area where an indoor soccer pitch had been set up, and Paige came after me. "You don't have to babysit me, you know," I said as we went.

"Who's babysitting? I love soccer."

Before I could strike up a conversation, we heard Tyler arguing with some kids who'd come in only a few minutes ago.

"You aren't our boss!" He glared up at a bigger kid

without a trace of intimidation on his face. "Ms. Hammel says everyone who wants to play can."

"Well, nobody wants you on their team," the kid said, his face twisted into the kind of scowl bullies seemed to perfect.

"I do," I said, raising my hands. "So why don't Tyler and I have our own team, and we play against you and whoever you want on your team. Sounds like that'll be fair."

The kid's hands curled into fists, and I wondered if all my good work today was going to get thrown away by a kid with a bad temper. I wouldn't hit him back, obviously, but I had no doubt the media could make it my fault.

"We got Mags and Larry," Tyler said. "That's four of us."

"I got eight," the kid said. "But the old guy should be able to make up the difference, right?"

Old?

"Five against eight sounds fair to me," Paige spoke up. She pulled her hair back from her face and called over to Candra, "Hey, let me borrow your shoes."

"You're gonna play soccer?" It was hard to say who was more skeptical, Tyler, or the smart-mouthed teenager leering at Paige.

She grinned at the older kid as she swapped out her dress shoes for a pair of sneakers. "No, I'm going to kick your ass at soccer."

I stared at her while the kids started shouting out positions to the others on the team. She stood up and caught me with my mouth hanging open like an idiot.

"What?"

"I just – I mean..." I stammered, "shit. I'm just surprised is all."

"That makes two of us," she said. The moment stretched out, then broke as she bent over to stretch. "You better be good at this, Union. I don't want to have to explain to the journalists over there why you're disappointing the kids."

I glanced toward the front doors, seeing the crowd for the first time. I wasn't sure if I wanted to be annoyed that Paige had called them here, or proud that she'd believed in me enough to bring in the media without really knowing how things were going to go, but either way I was now terrified. Partly because I knew if I made the smallest mistake, that's all anyone would focus on, but also because I didn't want to disappoint the kids. More than that, I didn't want to disappoint Paige.

FOURTEEN
PAIGE

I hadn't played soccer since intermural my sophomore year of college, but even with work, I'd managed to stay in shape. Reb, however, had spent the last few months drinking more than exercising, and while his body still looked fit as hell, he definitely wasn't a soccer player.

I sent the ball over to Mags with a neat little kick, then watched as she sent it sailing right into the make-shift goal.

"Yes!" She threw her hands into the air.

"Nice shot!" I held up my hand, and she slapped hers against it. "You're a natural."

She flushed, her eyes darting toward Reb. I didn't have to know her well to know that she had a crush on my musician.

No. No, *not* my musician. Reb wasn't mine.

And he sure as hell wasn't the reason why my face was suddenly hotter than it had been from physical exertion alone.

"Ringer," Reb said as he stopped behind me. He bent over, putting his hands on his knees. "You've played before."

"A little," I admitted with a grin. "Well, maybe more than a little."

"I'm glad you're on my side." He straightened, lifting his shirt to wipe the sweat from his face.

I tried not to stare at his stomach, and I definitely tried not to think about running my tongue over every one of those ridges.

I jumped a little when a whistle blew, and we looked over to see a large man waving the kids in for whatever was next on their schedule, his dark mocha skin gleaming with sweat.

"We have to go," Tyler said. "But this was the most fun I've ever had here."

Reb fist bumped him. "I had fun too." As the kids ran off, he added, "But I have a feeling it's going to come back to bite me in the ass in the morning."

"Why's that?" I asked as I waved a goodbye to Mags and Larry. "I think this is going to play well in the press."

"That's not what I meant," Reb said. He put his hands on the small of his back and leaned back, groaning as he stretched.

My stomach twisted, and I wondered if he made that sound during sex. "What did you mean then?" I asked, hoping to get my mind off of sex and Reb. That would end nowhere good.

"I'm a bit more out of shape than I realized." He

leaned to the left, grimacing as those muscles engaged. "I'm going to be stiff tomorrow."

The comment was innocuous enough, but I still couldn't stop my mind from changing it into something dirty.

Dammit.

"Hey, what are you doing tonight?"

I frowned as I looked over at him. "I didn't have anything scheduled for you, if that's what you're asking."

"It's not." He came over to stand in front of me. "I want to know what *you're* doing tonight."

"That's a bad idea," I said, shaking my head. "Whatever it is you're thinking, it's a bad idea."

"Really?" He gave me that grin again, like he knew that alone could make me wet. Then again, with as many women as he'd been with, he probably knew exactly what that smile did.

"Reb, you're my client. This is my job."

"And you promised me a reward if I behaved myself today," he reminded me.

"I did not." I scowled at him. "*You* said reward. *I* said–"

"That you'd make sure I 'got something for my troubles.'"

Shit.

I released a long breath. "Look, Reb–"

He held up a hand. "A friend of mine is having an art show. He's a photographer. My friends and I always go to showings and openings and all that, but this year, they have girlfriends. Well, one's married. Still hard to get used to... shit. Look, do you want to come with me?"

I almost laughed at the rambling, but he looked so earnest. Nothing like the drunk guy I first met. He'd gone from heated innuendo to a near-childlike eagerness, and I couldn't bring myself to treat him the same way I would have if he'd been drunk or lecherous.

"I suppose that would be okay," I said slowly. Spending time with him outside of work wasn't exactly professional, but going to some photography gallery was a lot better than any of the 'rewards' I'd been thinking he'd want.

"Don't sound so thrilled," Reb said wryly. "If you don't want to go–"

"I do," I cut him off. "I do."

His expression softened, and he reached out his hand. For a moment, I thought he was going to kiss me again, but instead, he plucked a leaf from my hair. "I'll pick you up at six."

I was going to tell him that I'd meet him at the gallery, but he walked away before I could say anything, leaving me with no choice but to stare at his ass as he went.

Really. No choice.

REB HADN'T GIVEN me a dress code, but I'd done a quick internet search for photography shows and found only one happening in the area tonight. It was for a photographer named Alix Wexler. Everything I saw told me this was black tie. Fortunately, the little black dress I'd worn for my college graduation a few months ago would work.

A part of me still felt underdressed as I walked into the gallery, my arm linked with Reb's. The faces I recognized here were some of the tops in their fields.

Dinah Weston was a prominent prosecutor who'd taken down a whole precinct of corrupt cops.

Stanley and Patty Driver owned some of the most prominent racehorses in the country, including three Kentucky Derby champions and two Breeders' Cup champions.

Erik Sanders was one of the wealthiest men under thirty in the city, and if the gossip columns I'd recently read were accurate, the beautiful blonde on his arm was Tanya Lacey, an employee of Branch Publishing and the woman responsible for an upcoming release that was getting rave reviews.

And we were walking right toward them.

Shit.

"Erik, Tanya," Reb greeted them both with a familiarity that said they knew each other from more than just a passing greeting at fundraisers.

Were *they* two of his friends?

Fuck.

Working for a large PR firm in a city like New York, I'd always expected to rub elbows with some of the upper crust, but it was one thing to meet them under professional circumstances, and something else altogether to be on the arm of someone like Reb, especially since it looked like we were anything other than working together.

"This is Paige Ryce," Reb said. "Paige, meet Erik Sanders and Tanya Lacey."

I held out a hand before either of them could initiate another type of greeting. I didn't know if they were huggers, but I did know that I didn't want to make things more awkward than they already were. Which, in hindsight, probably meant that I shouldn't have tried to shake their hands since they both looked like they were trying to hold back amusement that seemed to be directed more at Reb than me.

"Paige is the PR rep I told you about," Reb said. "She's amazing."

I couldn't stop a blush, and it only got worse when Erik raised an eyebrow, a questioning look in his bright blue eyes. Before I could decide whether or not I wanted him to say something, a handsome blond man approached. On his arm was a delicately beautiful woman who appeared to feel as out of place as I did.

"Reb." The man clasped Reb's hand and gave one of those half-hugs that only some men could pull off.

"Paige, this is Jace Randell and Savannah Birch."

I wasn't really into the art world, but even I had heard of Jace Randell, especially since rumor had it that he'd found a muse who inspired his newest series, sculptures rather than paintings. Sybil had tried to get tickets to the opening night of his show, but there'd been none to spare.

"Nice to meet you," Savannah said with a smile.

"You too." I glanced up at the guys who'd begun one of those conversations that came out of mutual experiences. "How do they all know each other?"

Tanya answered, "Reb and Erik met at Columbia. They were roommates until Reb left. Alix – the one whose show this is – is Erik's cousin."

"And Jace?"

The women exchanged looks, their cheeks flushing.

"They met at a club," Savannah said.

It sounded simple enough, but something in her light gray eyes made me think there was more to that statement than she was letting on. I wasn't about to press the issue though.

"There's the man of the hour." Erik's voice cut through our conversation as a dark-haired man who shared Erik's muscular build and chiseled jaw came toward us. He had to be Erik's cousin, and the photographer, Alix Wexler. I didn't know, however, who the tiny redhead tucked beneath his arm was.

"You look amazing," Savannah said as she hugged the newcomer. "Paige, this is Sine, Alix's wife. Sine, this is Paige Ryce. She's here with Reb."

"Lovely to meet you," Sine said with a smile.

"Likewise." I couldn't help but smile back. Between the orange-red curls, freckles, and Irish accent, I didn't imagine there were many people she couldn't charm.

"Is the morning sickness getting any better?" Tanya asked, sounding for all the world like a worried mother though I doubted there was much age difference between her and Sine.

Sine nodded. "Mam sent me a few local remedies that she swore by with my brothers and me and they've done the trick."

"And your doctor said it's safe for you to travel at the end of the month?"

Savannah sounded as protective of Sine as Tanya. I understood it though. Something about the young woman just brought it out.

"Sine and Alix are going to Ireland for a big wedding," Savannah explained. "They've already had a ceremony here, but Sine's mom wanted a ceremony in a church."

"Big Catholic family," Sine said with a smile. Her hand rested on her stomach in one of those absent gestures most pregnant women seemed to make. "Alix is convinced my father's going to kill him. Well, him or my brothers."

"You do have six of them," Tanya said with a soft laugh. "If Erik knocks me up, at least he doesn't have to worry about someone coming after him."

"Yes, he does," Savannah countered. "Because if he behaves like an ass, he'll have to deal with Sine and me."

I'd always been fine with family being just Mom and me, but seeing this group together, I felt a twinge of longing for a bigger family.

"So, Paige, you're here with Reb?" Tanya turned the conversation to me.

"Not like that," I quickly said. "I'm his public relations

rep." The trio exchanged knowing looks, and I shook my head. "What?"

Savannah and Sine looked at Tanya, who shrugged. "We've all been there."

"Been where?"

"Thinking that things were just professional between us and our men," Savannah said. "Tanya and Erik met over a book deal."

"Savannah's an art critic who was sent to do a story on Jace," Sine said.

"And Sine used to be Alix's assistant," Tanya finished up.

"Technically, I still am," Sine said. Her cheeks colored. "Just with a few...perks now."

We all laughed, but their words kept echoing back in my head as Reb came back to my side. The couples split off to mingle, and Reb led me through the gallery, his hand resting lightly on the small of my back.

"You seemed to be getting along well with the others," he said as we stopped in front of one of the first photographs.

"I like them," I said honestly. I didn't tell him that they thought he and I had more between us than work. They'd figure it out sooner or later, and I didn't see any reason to make things more awkward.

The picture in front of me was done in black and white, a slender model, nude save a pair of lace panties and a pair of handcuffs hanging from one wrist.

Oh. Okay.

The next photograph had the model from the neck down, a strip of silk across her breasts bringing the only color to the piece, a bright green that stood out starkly against the background.

"Does this bother you?" Reb asked, pitching his voice low enough that only I could hear it.

"Does what bother me?" I didn't look at him as I moved to the next picture.

The model was on her stomach again, but her panties were gone. The cut of the shot showed only the beginning swell of her ass, but it was clear she was naked. Her hands were tied together at the small of her back with the same bright cloth that had covered her breasts in the previous picture.

"I didn't know exactly what Alix's series was about, but he'd hinted that it was on the erotic side," Reb said. "I didn't think to ask if it would bother you."

I shook my head, willing my face not to betray me. There was no way I could let Reb know that, far from bothering me, the pictures turned me on in a way that was surprising. Not because I was attracted to the model, but because the subject matter touched something primal inside me.

The fourth picture was a close up of the model's mouth, lips cherry red around a ball gag. The fifth another close-up, but this time of her whole face. She wore a mask, and the gag was gone. The mask was gold, the rest black and white, but the simplicity of it made it stand out all the more. Her eyes were half-closed, her lips parted.

She was coming, I realized with a start. Either he'd hired someone who could fake it with amazing reality...or she'd really been coming. Which made me wonder if she'd done it herself, or if Alix had been the one...shit.

"I don't think I could do that," Reb said quietly. "Share my woman with the world."

My heart gave a funny skipping beat as I realized what he meant. "That's Sine."

"You didn't know?"

I shook my head, unable to tear my eyes from the photo.

"The whole series is her. That's why they're in black and white, so no one can see her hair or eye color," he explained. "Too easy to identify her."

"She doesn't seem the type," I said.

"The type to pose for erotic pictures?" Reb asked. "Or the type to get into BDSM?"

"Both," I admitted.

"Don't knock it until you've tried it," he said dryly as he moved to the next picture.

Tried it? The room was suddenly too hot, the air too thick. Was he simply telling me not to think I knew Sine after only a few minutes of conversation...or was he saying something else? Was he saying that this was what he was into? And that he wanted me to try it with *him*?

Fuck, fuck, *fuck*!

What had I gotten myself into?

And why did the idea of exploring these new, primal feelings appeal to me so much?

FIFTEEN
REB

Alix had told us that his series of pictures explored the juxtaposition between innocence and the erotic nature of BDSM, and that Sine had been his model, but, of course, I'd never even thought to tell Paige. Even if I had, I wasn't sure I would've been able to do it. Not after how things had gone with Mitzi.

If I was going to be completely honest with myself, I'd been caught between anticipation and anxiety from the moment I'd invited Paige to come with me. But then we were in the limo, and it was too late to change my mind. A part of me was grateful that the decision was no longer mine to make.

My friends had been polite to Paige, but as soon as she'd started talking to the other women, the guys had turned on me with smug smiles. I'd tried to blow them off, tell them that she was an employee of sorts, nothing more.

Then they'd reminded me that Tanya, Sine, and Savannah had all started in similar ways. I'd told them they were crazy.

Now, as we reached the end of the series, I was beginning to think they were right. With every new picture, the tension between the two of us grew. Neither of us had said anything since those first few portraits, but she studied each new one we came to. The one with the flogger resting on the small of Sine's back. The one where the only color was the pink handprints on her ass.

Alix really had found his muse with Sine. I'd been skeptical of her, both before she left, and even more when she'd come back, but I could see it now. How good the two of them were together.

I'd meant what I said to Paige though. I didn't understand how Alix could display the pictures for the world to see. Then again, just because we were both Doms didn't mean the same things got us off. For example, exhibitionism wasn't my thing, but it apparently got things going for Alix and Sine.

I hoped he knew how lucky he was to have found someone like her. Not that I found her attractive beyond aesthetic appreciation. I didn't envy him the girl, but I did envy what they had. The freedom to be who he wanted to be, to want what he wanted and not be judged for it.

I shook off the self-pitying thoughts and smiled at Alix as Paige and I walked over to where he and Sine were talking to Congressman Powers. I gave the older man a polite nod as he said his goodbyes, then turned back to my friend.

"Amazing," I said, leaning in to give him a hard clap on the back. "I knew you were talented, but damn. This is the best work I've ever seen you do."

"It's all because of her," Alix said, kissing the top of Sine's head.

She gave him an exasperated look. "Take the compliment, love."

Erik and Tanya came up then, and while I knew I should probably hang around a bit, the combination of the photos and having Paige next to me for the past hour was either going to drive me to drink...or do something else that probably wasn't a good idea.

Which meant I needed to get Paige away from me.

"Ready to go?" I asked.

She looked surprised by the question but nodded in agreement. I quickly said our goodbyes, slid my arm around her waist, and walked us out to where the valet was waiting.

It didn't take long for us to get into the limo, but we stopped almost immediately when we pulled onto the highway.

So much for getting away from Paige.

"Is something wrong?" She broke the silence with a question and a hand on my forearm. "You looked like you were enjoying yourself, and then you suddenly wanted to leave."

"Nothing's wrong," I said as I turned toward her. Her hand dropped from my arm to land on my knee, burning through the denim.

Fuck it.

I cupped her face in my hands and kissed her, pouring everything in me into her. Our first kiss had been just as rash, just as impetuous, but unless she told me to stop, I didn't intend to let her go this time. If I was going to fuck up my life even more than it already was, at least I'd get something out of it.

For a moment, she stiffened, and I worried that she was going to pull away, but then her mouth softened, lips parted. When her hands grabbed the front of my jacket, I slapped my hand against the button to close the tinted window between the front seat and the back area. I was planning on taking full advantage of whatever was keeping us stuck in traffic, but unlike Alix, I didn't intend for anyone but me to see Paige this way.

She pushed my jacket off my shoulders, her hands greedy as she grabbed my ass and then yanked my shirt out of the back of my pants. I nipped her bottom lip, then sucked it into my mouth, the taste of her going straight to my cock. I felt like a teenager again, my hands running over her dress, learning every curve of her body.

The limo started to move again, but it was slow enough that I barely acknowledged it. I was more concerned with getting Paige stretched out underneath me and seeing if those legs looked as good as they felt.

"Fuck, Reb," she gasped as I kissed my way down her neck. "Are you sure this is a good idea?"

No.

"Yes."

I moved further down her body, settling between her legs even as she grabbed my shoulders.

"What are you—"

I pulled her panties to the side and licked her.

"Fuck!"

I pressed my mouth against her pussy, my hands on her hips to keep her in place. She gasped and cursed, writhing as I ran my tongue over her sensitive skin, then around her clit. Fuck. I'd never imagined how hot it could be to see someone as polished as her completely come apart. I needed to make her come, and then we could decide if I'd go upstairs to her place or she'd come to mine to continue this.

It didn't take much, telling me she'd been wound as tight as me. I moved the tip of my tongue in rapid flicks over her clit, and then she was crying out my name so loud that I doubted even the sound-proofed barrier could keep the driver from hearing her. Not that I minded. He needed to know that she was with me. She was *mine*.

I moved back up her body to take her mouth, my erection rubbing against the space between her legs. Then I shifted, and she stiffened, pulling back.

"Sorry, am I crushing you?" I pushed myself off of her.

She shook her head as she smoothed down her skirt. "No, no, I was just...I mean, we shouldn't..."

"Hey, it's okay," I said, pressing my forehead against hers. "I'm not expecting anything."

She looked flustered. More so than I'd ever seen her. I reached out and tucked some hair behind her ear. She didn't flinch, but she didn't lean into my touch either.

"I'm serious, Paige. I wouldn't pressure you into anything you didn't want to do." She still wouldn't meet my eyes. "Was your last ex a jerk or something?"

She shook her head and offered me a half-smile. "No, it's nothing like that."

"What then?" I asked, mostly because I wanted to know, but also because talking would help keep my mind off of my throbbing case of blue balls. "You're some kind of ice queen? Don't want to lose your virginity in the back of a limo?"

I said it as a joke, but then I registered her expression. Her wide eyes. The way the color drained from her face.

Fuck.

Suddenly, the door opened, and the driver was smiling down at us.

"I'm going now." Her voice was hoarse.

I just nodded, too shocked to say anything, not even when she climbed out of the car and refused to look at me. A virgin? Had I seriously almost just deflowered my PR rep in the back of a limo?

I needed to get my life straightened up, and fast, because if I didn't, it was going to spin so out of control that no PR would fix it.

I STRUMMED my fingers across the strings of my guitar, not really trying to play a specific chord, but rather just hearing the different notes and trying to figure out where they should go. It always sounded strange when I tried to explain it that way. People tended to get it in their heads that music was composed in a certain way, but everyone had different ways of doing things.

I hadn't heard the music in my head for too long, and it wasn't back yet, but I could feel it coming. Like something on the tip of my tongue, or in the back of my mind. Something not quite remembered.

Still, it gave me something to concentrate on instead of thinking about Paige and what I'd almost done last night.

A virgin. She was a virgin.

That was the last thing I needed. Even if I held back, denied the things I really wanted, it was a lot of pressure, being someone's first. My first time had been with my high school girlfriend, and she'd been a virgin too. It hadn't been bad, but awkward, and when we'd broken up a few months later, she'd yelled at me about getting what I wanted from her and then throwing her aside.

Between that and what happened with Mitzi, I was more determined than ever to stick with finding subs at Gilded Cage, the BDSM club my friends and I frequented. No more relationships, and definitely not sleeping with any virgins. Hell, I didn't even want someone who'd fucked several guys but was new to the BDSM world.

Even if the thought of someone else teaching Paige all the ways pain and pleasure could come together set my teeth on edge. I'd never thought of myself as a proprietary guy, but with her...

It turned out that working on music really wasn't doing much to keep my mind off of Paige.

By evening, I was ready to either drink myself stupid or go over Paige's and fuck her until neither of us could think straight. Fortunately, I was saved from doing either of those stupid things because Erik called.

In less than a half-hour, all three guys were sitting in my living room.

"Here," Erik said as he held out a sheaf of papers. "I just finished the revisions for *The Muse*. Thought you and the guys would like to take a look. You took off last night before I had a chance to give it to you."

"They're really putting a rush on it," Jace said. "Trying to get it out by the end of the year. Savannah said it's unusual to get two books published so close together."

Erik nodded. "Branch wants to use my books to try to see if they can compete with how quickly independent authors get their books out."

"I gave Sine my copy this morning," Alix said. "I'm thanking you in advance for the night I'm going to have when I get home. Seriously, that shit you write, it's like fucking catnip for her. She read *Heat of the Sun* on our honeymoon, and I swear, I thought she was going to break my dick."

I flipped through the book, then set it aside to read later. I'd never go around telling people that I was a fan of Erika Summers erotica, but Erik was a damn good writer, and there were worse things to have for a guilty pleasure.

"How are things going with Paige?" Jace asked. "The two of you looked good together."

"It's not like that." I shook my head.

"Yeah, we all said that, remember?" Alix laughed. "Come on, man, you watched all three of us fall hard. We know what it looks like."

"Whatever," I mumbled, glaring at him.

"Don't fight it," Jace advised. "Trust us, it doesn't work."

"There's nothing to fight," I insisted. "We're strictly professional."

Except for last night in the limo.

Alix raised an eyebrow. "Bullshit."

I scowled. "Like hell it is."

"I saw the way the two of you looked at each other," he persisted.

"Look," I said with a sigh, "I don't know what you think you saw, but it's not there. Sure, she's attractive, but I'm not looking to get involved with anyone. Not after what happened the last time."

"For all you know, she could be into the same stuff," Jace offered. "You'll never know until you at least try."

"She's a virgin," I snapped. "That's the last thing I need."

Erik closed his eyes. "Please tell me you didn't do something stupid. Tanya really likes her."

Shit. The last thing I needed was them getting on my case. They were supposed to be on my side. "We fooled around, but when I found out she was a virgin, it didn't go any further."

"That's not the stupid I meant," he said. He opened his eyes, a disapproving expression on his face. "You acted like an ass, didn't you? You found out she was a virgin, and instead of talking to her about it, you freaked out and either said something asinine, or you said nothing at all."

Okay, he had me there. The *ice queen* comment hadn't been meant cruelly, but it wasn't a nice thing to say.

"So what?" I said sullenly.

Erik looked at Jace, then Alix, who both gave him a half-hearted shrug as if to say *go ahead*. "If any of you tell anyone what I'm about to say, I'll kill you." He paused a moment to let his threat sink in. "When Paige and I first had sex, I didn't know she was a virgin until…well, you get the idea. And I freaked out, accusing her of intentionally hiding things from me, telling her that I didn't want that responsibility. I almost lost the best thing that's ever happened to me because I didn't just talk to her."

"Communication is key," Jace added his two cents. "Erik's right about that."

"Hell, yes," Alix agreed. "You saw how miserable I was

when Sine was gone, and it all could've been avoided if I'd just talked to her, given her the benefit of the doubt."

I sighed and leaned back. "I don't know. Seems like a big risk."

"It is," Erik admitted. "But I know that all three of us would agree that it's worth it."

"Hell, yes," Alix and Jace chorused.

I'd brought them over here to keep myself from drinking, but now, alcohol was looking even better than ever.

What the hell was I supposed to do now?

SIXTEEN
PAIGE

If I thought about it, I probably could have come up with a time where I'd been more mortified than I had been Saturday night, but I couldn't think of anything off the top of my head. I told myself that wasn't because a memory didn't exist, but rather because I'd long since buried it.

I wished I could do the same with what happened in the limo. The tension between us at the show had been bearable, but the moment he'd kissed me, everything had turned upside-down.

I should have remembered that no matter how good-looking Reb was, no matter how much I might be attracted to him, he would never be the sort of man I could trust. Not to that extent anyway.

I would do my job, and I would do it well. I'd give Sybil no cause to regret giving it to me. Once I could claim Reb's new, good image as a product of my hard work, Sybil could feel confident giving me more. I could see it all ahead of me. Lots of nights working late. No social life. No men. No friends.

It was everything I'd ever wanted.

And if I kept telling myself that, I might believe it one day.

I looked down at the message I'd gotten from Reb twenty minutes ago. *Late start. Let yourself in.*

I didn't want to think about why Reb'd had a late night. He'd looked so horrified at the realization that I was a virgin that I suspected he'd gone out yesterday to find someone more experienced to fuck. Someone who didn't come across as so desperate and needy.

A flush of shame colored my cheeks, and I pushed those thoughts down as far as I could. I was done thinking about him that way. From here on out, he was only going to be a client. Mr. Union. Nothing else.

I knocked first, just in case Reb was within earshot of the door, but when he didn't answer, I let myself in as he'd instructed. I supposed he felt safe enough with the security doors downstairs, the doorman, security detail, and the keycard necessary to get to his floor. I couldn't imagine living anywhere in New York City where I could leave the door unlocked like that.

"Re – Mr. Union?" I called as I entered the apartment. No answer. I walked a bit farther in, wondering if I'd find him passed out on the couch. The place was clean, which surprised me. I hoped that meant he was still sober.

I suddenly realized that I could hear the shower running, and a flood of heat hit me along with the memories of what his skin looked like wet. Those tattoos. That skin. Those muscles.

"Dammit," I cursed softly.

I needed to find a distraction.

Fortunately, fate seemed to take some sympathy on me, and I spotted something on the end table next to the couch. *The Muse* by Ericka Summers. I knew that name, but couldn't quite place why. Not that it mattered, I would've read pretty much anything at the moment if it meant I could stop thinking about the fact that Reb was naked and wet only a few yards away.

I sat down and picked up the manuscript, making a mental note to ask how Reb ended up with it in the first place...then I remembered that this was a distraction so I could stay professional. It was none of my business how he'd gotten this from Ms. Summers.

I flipped it open to the acknowledgment page. *To my one and only muse. You are my life.*

It was simple, and even more beautiful for the simplicity.

I turned to the first place and started to read.

The sound of the whip came a split second before it struck, a sharp crack that echoed off the walls. Her whimper was a softer sound, but it still made his cock even harder. It was art, what he did, though most wouldn't see it that way. Art could be sensual, even bordering on sexual, but once erotic was the word used to describe it, people started getting twitchy.

He frowned. The people here appreciated his talents,

but if he couldn't concentrate, he couldn't deliver, and they'd start looking elsewhere. Not that he needed the job, per se, but having him here was mutually beneficial. He drew a crowd for the club and was able to create his art in a safe environment. He could never let anyone see his face. His identity had to remain a secret, and this was the best way for that to happen...

It didn't take me long to get caught up in the world of Maximillian von Strauss, the Dominant billionaire recluse, and the object of his obsession and affection, reluctant club hostess Chastity Powell. Sure, her name was a bit on-the-nose, and alpha billionaire romances weren't usually my preferred genre, but the writing was amazing, the characters likable even with their flaws. Despite my preconceived notions of the romance genre – particularly the erotic vein – *The Muse* had substance.

And the sex...one scene was hotter than the next.

Max had told her when they'd first come together that he intended to have all of her, and she was now starting to realize exactly what that meant.

She was naked and face-down, head turned to the side, silk sheets cool beneath her body. Her arms and legs were spread wide, each bound to the four corners of the bed. The restraints were soft, which she had learned meant whatever he had planned for her would make her try to break free. The thought didn't frighten her though, not beyond the small bite of anticipatory fear. She knew she had only to say the word, and he'd release her.

She heard the door open but didn't speak. Over the past

few days, she had learned what he expected of her. He liked to talk, but only wanted her to answer questions, not give voice to anything else unless it was to stop the scene. And she didn't want that.

She felt the bed dip as he climbed between her legs. She shuddered as his finger slid inside her. She was wet, of course. She was always wet around him.

Something cool and smooth brushed against her entrance, and she sucked in a breath as a thin dildo slid inside her. It wasn't nearly as large around as he was, barely larger than his finger, but every nerve in her body was on edge, ready for whatever he had planned. She suspected what it would be, but it wasn't until he removed the toy from her pussy and spread her cheeks that she knew she was right.

"I'm going to take your ass tonight, Chastity," he said quietly. "There will be times when it will hurt, but if you can bear it, I promise you an experience more intense than anything you've had before."

She nodded, but it was an acknowledgment rather than permission. By not saying her safe word, she gave consent.

"Ahhh..." It was half a moan, half some other sound entirely, but it wasn't a conscious choice she made, simply the noise that escaped as Max eased the slick plastic shaft into her ass. She felt a faint burn, but nothing painful. More uncomfortable than anything else.

And then his fingers were in her pussy, relentlessly stroking her to an orgasm even as he fucked her ass with the dildo. She whimpered and gasped, closing her eyes to allow the sensations to wash over her. For an eternity, he stretched her ass even as he took her to the edge again and again, never letting her fall over it. She didn't beg, knowing he'd tell her if he wanted her to, but it was almost impossible not to plead with him to let her come.

Without warning, her ass and pussy were both empty, and she felt the heat of him as he leaned over her back and put his mouth against her ear.

"Once my cock starts filling your ass, you can come as much as you want, say whatever you want. I want you to come apart underneath me, holding nothing back."

She nodded again, body trembling with its need for release. When the head of his cock pressed against her anus, she knew she'd come the moment he penetrated her, pain or not. She needed it. Needed him.

He leaned forward and–

"Find anything interesting to read?"

SEVENTEEN
REB

I wished I had a camera. Not just because seeing Paige jump and look guilty when I spoke was one of the funniest things I'd seen in a long time, but because I wanted to lock in the memory of finding her like this.

Her cheeks were flushed, pupils dilated so wide that only a thin ring of blue-green was visible. She was embarrassed now, but I doubted that was the only reason she couldn't look at me.

She was turned on. For a moment, I thought it was because she'd been thinking about me being in the shower, but then she set something on the table as she stood and I realized what she'd been doing.

Dammit, Erik.

If she hadn't been reading that book, I probably could have let it go. I still *should* have let it go. We had to keep things professional. That was the only way this was going to work. We had to ignore any lingering chemistry between us. If there was even any left after the way I'd put her off the other night.

But my ability to say no to temptation was part of the reason I was in this mess in the first place.

"Like it?" I asked, raising an eyebrow. "I can let the author know if there was anything in particular you thought was...stimulating."

"You know her?" Paige asked, glancing toward the manuscript. She frowned, as if her question bothered her. "Never mind. It's not important. I was just bored waiting for you, and it was there."

"You looked like you were enjoying it." I couldn't resist. "I could come back later if you want to be alone..."

"Don't be an asshole," she snapped.

Damn, she was hot when she was pissed. Made me want to push her even more, see just how much she could take. That was the part of BDSM that attracted me the most. Testing limits. Not necessarily pain, but comfort levels.

Like going down on her in the back of a limo.

"Come on, Paige, no need to be embarrassed. I had it for a reason." I walked toward her, knowing every step was a worse idea than the last.

But I didn't stop.

"Because you...*know* Erika Summers?"

I grinned. "Is that jealousy I hear?"

She glared at me, crossing her arms, as if that would offer any sort of deterrent. If anything, it made matters worse because it drew my attention to her full breasts. I hadn't gotten nearly enough of my fill of them.

"We already went down this road, Mr. Union," she said, lifting her chin. "And I know you don't want to go there again, so let's just stick with business."

"And if I'd rather focus on pleasure?" The words just popped out, but when I saw her blush again, I didn't regret them. My friends' words echoed in my head, louder than they'd been all day. I wanted her, despite what I knew, and despite all the reasons I'd given myself why I shouldn't.

"Reb..."

My name was a warning, but the fact that she'd called me *Reb* instead of *Mr. Union* made me think that she wasn't as opposed to the connection as she tried to seem.

"How far did you get? I'm sure Erik has all sorts of new ideas in there for you to think about."

"Erik?" Her eyes widened.

Shit.

"As in your friend, one of the wealthiest men under thirty, Erik Sanders?"

I could tell by her face that she'd put it all together before she even finished the question.

He was going to kick my ass.

"*He's* Erika Summers?" She looked down at the manuscript again. "That's how he and Tanya met, isn't it? The book deal wasn't for some memoir or how to succeed in business thing. It was for *Heat of the Sun*."

"You can't tell anyone," I said, making my face as serious

as possible. "The only people who know are us guys, Sine, Savannah, Tanya obviously, and one or two other people at Branch Publishing. Even Erik's sisters don't know."

"I won't," she promised. A flare of understanding lit in her eyes. "Is he into...I mean, him and Tanya..." Her cheeks flamed red. "You said Alix and Sine..."

"It's not as uncommon as a lot of people think," I said, the muscles in my shoulders tensing. "Does it make you think less of them?"

My question sounded like a natural follow up, but tension hummed through my body as I waited for her answer.

"No," she said, giving me a steady look. "I may be a virgin, but I'm not a prude. I believe that, as long as things are between consenting adults, it's not anyone else's business what goes on, and certainly not anyone's place to judge."

I could see that she believed every word she said, but I knew all too well how words were easy enough to say when nothing was on the line. When I'd first talked to Mitzi about it, she'd acted like she was fine with it, but later, things changed.

"So, your opinion is that it's fine for other people, but nothing you'd want to explore?" I mentally cursed myself as soon as the question was out of my mouth. That sounded like I was propositioning her.

She drew herself up to her full height and gave me the sort of look that said I'd gone too far. "I think we should stick with business-related conversation."

I nodded even as my head agreed with my treacherous cock that they were more interested in getting an answer than talking business. I might have been trying all weekend to convince myself that I didn't want to sleep with a virgin, but I'd also been coming up with some pretty good arguments about why it just might be more appealing than I realized.

Like the fact that I'd never have to wonder if another man had been able to make her come the same way, or if she was comparing me to some previous lover. For whatever amount of time we were together, I'd be able to know that I was the only man she'd ever given herself to. I'd be her first in every sense, the one to show her all the different ways she could find pleasure, to teach her the ways to please me.

I could implant myself so firmly in her mind that every other man who came after me would never be able to live up to the standard I'd set. She'd be completely and indelibly mine.

EIGHTEEN
PAIGE

How had I thought I'd be able to talk to him like nothing had happened? Every time I looked at him, all I could think of was what it had felt like to kiss him, to touch him. The memory of his hands on my body, his mouth...it made every cell heat up, every nerve buzz with electricity.

Maybe coming here hadn't been a complete mistake, but reading that book had been. The moment I realized what I'd been reading, I should have stopped. Not because there was something wrong with it, but because being turned on right now was making things even more difficult than usual.

"I talked to some people from work about forty minutes ago, and they've been analyzing the coverage of you and the kids. You're trending in the right direction, but that alone isn't going to turn things completely around. What we need to do is show people that the negative press is the fluke, not this. They need to see that you're a good guy who did something stupid."

"And you have some ideas of how to make me a good guy?"

The question should have been flippant, especially considering he'd essentially been teasing me from the moment he'd come into the living room, but something under his words told me he wasn't being as glib as he tried to sound.

Despite the fact that looking at him made me feel things I didn't want to feel, I turned toward him. He needed to know this. "I don't need to *make* you into a good guy. You already are one. I just need to get others to see it."

He gave me a puzzled look. "You think I'm a good person? Even after–"

I sighed, my resolve to keep things professional already being put to the test. "You made some bad choices after your break-up, and did some stupid things, but that doesn't make you a bad guy."

"Yeah, but the other night–"

I held up a hand to stop him. "We don't need to talk about that. It was impulsive, and the result of spending time together in a...*charged* environment. Neither of which will be happening again anytime soon."

"I'm sorry I called you an ice queen and then joked about the whole virginity thing."

I'd never really thought of myself as a person who was easily embarrassed, but this was getting to be a habit. "Reb, seriously, it's okay. Let's just get to work."

He opened his mouth like he was going to argue, then closed it again when I glared at him. He nodded. "All right."

"Good." I turned away so he couldn't see the relief on my face. Rehashing things would only make working with Reb more awkward. "The key to keeping the press on your side rather than them spinning things into a negative light is to make the experiences personal."

"And how do we do that?"

"By figuring out what matters to you." I did my best to fix on my professional face before I turned back to him. I would've used the same strategy with any client in a similar situation, but asking these questions of Reb felt a lot more intimate than it should have. "Obviously, music, but that's the part of you people already know. We need to show them the man behind the music."

He ran his fingers through his hair, flicking little droplets of water down onto his shirt. "What if music is all I am?" He gave me a sideways glance. "I haven't been able to write for more than six months. What if I can't ever write again and that's the legacy I leave? A stalled career and bad decisions?"

"I'm going to make sure that doesn't happen." I crossed over to him and put a hand on his arm. "I can't help with the music, but we're going to fix it so that these past couple months are only going to be a blip in an otherwise reputable career."

"How?"

I took a step back and let my hand fall to my side. "Tell

me about yourself. The things you like. What you're passionate about."

His eyes locked with mine for a moment, and I swallowed hard at the intensity I saw there. Then he was moving, turning away so he could walk over to the couch and take a seat. I stayed standing.

"I thought you did your research on me."

"That can tell me facts, not beliefs."

He studied me for a moment before answering. "My mom was a teacher's assistant when she was married to my dad, so I've always had a weak spot for educational charities."

"I've heard your mother talk about her time as a TA," I said. "She doesn't explain though why she was working when her family is certainly well-off enough that she doesn't need a regular job."

"My grandparents didn't approve of her marriage to my dad," he explained, his tone casual, as if this was something he'd gotten used to saying. "They eloped, actually. He was getting ready to be shipped overseas, and he wanted to make sure she was taken care of if something happened to him."

"He was military?" I hadn't been able to find much about Reb's father, only that he was dead.

Reb nodded. "Special Forces. We weren't allowed to know much about what he did, and even after he died on an assignment." His mouth quirked in a sad smile. "I was sixteen."

My heart squeezed, and it was hard not to go to him

then. To comfort him. To make him think of only me. "Oh, Reb, I'm so sorry."

"Thank you," he said. "Losing him almost destroyed my mom. She's always been proud of him, but she can't talk about him much. Even after all this time, she hasn't gotten over him."

My heart broke even more for him, and for his mom. My mom had raised me alone, and my father had never been more than biology and a cautionary tale. She'd never dated anyone, barely showed any interest in romance, and she sure as hell hadn't pined over any of the 'rock gods' she'd slept with.

I couldn't imagine loving someone so much that the loss of them changed my world forever. Well, I loved my mother, but that was different. Kids expected to outlive their parents. But when someone made a vow to love someone until death parted them, they never wanted to think that they'd have anything other than a lifetime to fulfill it.

"My older sister is terrified that her daughters will join the military someday. My younger sister works with Doctors Without Borders in some of the worst places in the world because she thinks that's what my dad would have wanted." He stared down at his hands thoughtfully. "A few months after my dad died, I talked to a recruiter. I started working out so I'd be physically ready as soon as I turned eighteen, but I kept it to myself. I didn't want to hurt my mom, but I felt like this was how I could honor my father."

I moved closer but resisted the urge to touch him.

"Two months before my birthday, I was driving home from a party, and a drunk driver ran a red light. The crash didn't do much damage, but I was stuck in the car. There was a fire, and I couldn't get out. A guy driving by stopped and pulled me out before the car caught fire, but because he had to rush, he accidentally dislocated my left shoulder." Reb's hand rubbed his shoulder as if he could still feel the pain. "It was bad enough that it ended up keeping me from enlisting." He looked up at me. "I've never told anyone that."

I tried not to feel warm at the admission. It didn't mean anything more than he found me easy to talk to. Like how someone might feel comfortable talking to a therapist. Nothing more.

I brought the conversation back to the matter at hand, not wanting to risk things going from personal to intimate. "I think I have enough to work with. I'll have something set up for the end of the week."

"Oh, okay. Good." He stood, a troubled expression on his face for a few moments before disappearing. "I'll keep the weekend free."

"Friday too," I said. "I'll let you know as soon as I have something scheduled."

He walked me to the door, opening it partway before stopping. "We should do something this weekend. Something besides work. I'd like to take you somewhere. A club. We can have some drinks. Dance. Loosen up some."

I started shaking my head as soon as I realized what he

was asking. "I don't think that's a good idea. Professional, remember?"

"Think of it as a reward for hard work." He gave me that irresistible smile. Not the plastic one he threw out to reporters, or even the polite one he had for fans. No, this was the smile that had made me melt into a puddle of malleable goo.

I sighed. "Let's see how things go first."

He beamed, and I mentally cursed myself for not being able to say no to him. As I left, I wasn't sure if I wanted him to do well on his next project or not. One option was definitely safer for me, but rooting for him to excel wasn't only for professional reasons. It wasn't even all because I wanted him to do well.

Even though I'd given myself repeated warnings, I still wanted him.

NINETEEN
REB

I slid my hand over the curve of her hip, then dug my fingers into her flesh to hold her in place as I slid inside. She was tight and wet and hot, everything I'd imagined and better. She moaned and whimpered, the sounds making me even harder. Everything had been building toward this moment, all the dancing around and flirting, the tension.

I reached out and took her hair, wrapping it around my fist. I pulled her head up so that I could see her expression in the mirror in front of us. So I could watch every nuance...

I jerked awake, my heart racing and my breathing ragged. The central air pumped cold air into the guest room, but my skin was still damp with sweat. I tossed the sheet aside, glowering down at the erection tenting my boxers. Of course, I had to have an erotic dream the night before I was supposed to see Paige again. Because it wasn't difficult enough to not get a fucking hard-on whenever I was around her.

I stretched my arm out and snagged my phone from the bedside table. The alarm I'd set was still ten minutes from going off, but I knew that it wouldn't do any good for me to lounge in bed until it did. It made more sense for me to spend a little extra time in the shower. My hand wasn't exactly the attention my cock would've preferred, but it was the quickest way to solve my problem.

PAIGE'S TEXT had only given me a time and an address, not an explanation of what the place was or what I'd be doing, so I was surprised when the taxi dropped me off in front of The Kamden McBride Foundation, a private organization that worked with veterans.

How had Paige figured out that I was connected to this place? No one knew about my yearly anonymous donations. I hadn't even told my mom or sisters about it. I supposed Paige could've followed the money, but that would've taken some serious resources. Unnecessary ones at that since all she would've needed to do was ask me. It didn't fit with what I knew about her. And Chester couldn't have told her because he managed me, not my money, and certainly not my inheritance.

As long as Paige didn't reveal my monetary contributions, I wouldn't push the issue, but I was curious.

She was leaning against the front of the building when I arrived, absorbed in something on her phone, and I allowed myself a moment to appreciate how her skirt showed off her legs. Her hair was pulled up behind her head, a few waves left to frame her face, and the memory of my dream hit me hard. I could almost feel the silk of her hair across my palm.

This was going to be a long day.

But, apparently, a good one.

I didn't have much time for things to think about my dream, or about the club I'd invited her to, because as soon as we walked into the building, she put me to work.

I talked to every veteran there, thanked them for their service, listened to the things that concerned them. And I shared about my father, how I remembered what it was like to say goodbye when he left for tours, somehow knowing – even as a kid – that he might not come back. I told them about the first time I remembered going to the airfield to pick him up, about answering the door when a pair of officers came to tell us that he wouldn't be coming home again.

Talking about it wasn't as difficult as I'd imagined.

I played requests, everything from "Happy Birthday" to "God Bless America" to "Sweet Home Alabama," and for the first time in a long time – with the exception of playing for those kids – music was fun. And not just for me either. Everyone was smiling and laughing, including Paige and me.

For hours, I didn't think about all the stupid things I'd done or what else I was going to need to do to get my career back on track. I even managed to keep from thinking too much about how much I wanted to drag Paige somewhere private and show her how good it would be to submit to me.

As things wound down, she and I finally had a couple minutes to stand back and breathe.

"Thank you," I said quietly.

"Just doing my job."

I reached over and grabbed her hand. Her eyes widened, but she didn't pull away. "No, you could have set me up with some flashy publicity stunts and considered your job complete. You didn't just gloss over what I'd done, give it a Band-Aid. You found things that I'd actually enjoy and be good at."

She shrugged. "I didn't need to change who you are, or re-vamp your image. People just needed a little reminder of why they liked you in the first place."

"I needed the reminder too," I said, squeezing her hand. "Thank you, again."

For a brief moment, I thought we'd address the connection we couldn't seem to shake, but then her phone rang, and it was over.

She turned to take the call, and I started to make my goodbyes. By the time she was done, I had a taxi waiting, and the two of us walked out together. I tried not to think of how similar this was to what had happened just a week before. I knew I couldn't kiss her this time, and not only because the taxi didn't offer us the same privacy. If I was going to see if the two of us could be something more, then I needed to play this right.

Which meant, as we pulled up in front of Paige's apartment building, I leaned toward her. "About my reward..."

TWENTY
PAIGE

Dress sexy, he'd said. He asked me to a club, told me to dress sexy, and then let the taxi carry him away. I'd spent most of the night wondering if I'd imagined it or if it had been some impulsive gesture that he'd immediately regretted. Then, this morning, he sent me a text, telling me when he'd be by to pick me up.

And I'd spent the rest of the day switching between trying to talk myself into canceling things and finding the perfect outfit.

By the time I finished my light dinner, I'd decided to see things through and then settled on a dress for the night. The most daring dress I'd ever owned. A deep, rich green, it made my eyes pop and my skin glow. It clung to every curve, had a daring neckline, and the length was short enough that I'd never been comfortable wearing it before. I'd never had anywhere to go where it'd seemed appropriate. Certainly not any work function.

This, though, wasn't a work function. It didn't matter that Reb had joked about it being a reward for his good behavior. We both knew we were crossing a line here. Going to an art show had been getting close to unprofessional behavior even before the incident in the limo, but a club...even before he'd said to dress sexy, I'd known it meant something more, though what, exactly, I didn't know.

I buzzed him up and smoothed down some non-existent wrinkles as I waited for him to come to the door. My stomach was in knots, reminding me why I'd previously avoided this sort of thing, and the fact that I thought Reb was worth all this trouble freaked me out almost as much as the date itself. Maybe more, if I was being totally honest with myself.

Then I was opening the door and praying that I didn't embarrass myself. The stunned expression on his face as he saw me calmed my nerves a bit. It wasn't the type of shock that came with a condescending *I never thought you could look that good* statement, but rather the same sort of breathless *oh* that I had going on when I saw him.

He wore fitted pants that were either leather or denim but did amazing things for him either way. His shirt was short-sleeved and tight, emphasizing the muscles I'd felt the previous week while showing off the tattoos on his arms. He definitely looked more the bad-boy rock star tonight than the wealthy philanthropist, and even though I didn't want it to, my body tightened in response.

"Damn..." he finally said.

His eyes had darkened to a shade of purple I hadn't realized was even possible, and the heat in them turned my insides to liquid.

"Not so bad yourself," I admitted, my voice shakier than I liked.

He grinned at that and held out a hand. "Shall we?"

I placed my hand in his and tried not to shiver. His fingers wrapped around mine, his grip firm, but not too tight. Neither of us spoke as we made our way down to the car he had waiting. It wasn't a limo, but it was definitely nicer than anything I could've afforded.

Once we were settled into the back, the driver pulled away from the curb, and Reb poured me a glass of champagne. I wasn't much of a drinker, but I appreciated the chance to have something to take the edge off.

"After we get there," he broke the silence, "if you're uncomfortable, if you want to go, just tell me."

I frowned. "Uncomfortable? I wasn't raised Amish, Reb." Why did people always assume that just because I was a virgin or because I wasn't a social person, that I was sheltered?

He finished the rest of his drink and set his glass aside. "I can tell." His eyes sparkled. "The dress gives it away."

I laughed, and some of the tension in my chest eased. Not all of it though, because I was still trying to figure out why Reb thought a club would make me uncomfortable.

As soon as we passed through the short foyer and into the club itself, his reasoning became clear.

Because this wasn't just some swanky private club; it

was a sex club. Specifically, an S&M club, or a BDSM club, as was more accurate.

"Paige?"

I looked up to see Reb watching me with a concerned expression on his face. I raised an eyebrow. "Are you going to show me around, or should I find someone else to do it?"

His expression darkened, and he stepped closer to me. "You're here with me, Paige."

A little thrill went through me at his words. They should have bothered me, but something about them told me it wasn't meant as an insult. It didn't take a genius to figure out his role here. He carried himself with the sort of power that demanded attention, and it wasn't only in his professional life. He drew people to him, and I wasn't the only one who saw it, who felt it. Thanks to popular entertainment over the last few years, I knew the title for someone like that was Dominant.

He took my hand and tucked it tight against his side, taking me farther into the club. I felt eyes on us, and it wasn't just my imagination. People moved around him, smiling, dipping their heads. The looks I got were more curious than hostile, but there were a few people – men and women alike – who didn't seem too pleased with my presence. No one said anything though.

Not that I would have noticed it if they had. A slow, seductive beat pulsed through the club, but it wasn't the music that had my attention. No, I was trying to act like seeing leather-clad, chain-wearing couples grinding against each other was normal for me. Like the threesome on the stage wasn't anything new.

Both men were bare-chested and wore black leather pants, but that was where the similarities ended. One was well over six feet tall and solid, like a linebacker. He was dark-haired, with a square, blunt-looking face. The other was shorter and slimmer, with pale hair and a narrow face.

The woman was tiny, probably even smaller than Sine, with piles of golden blonde hair, and pierced nipples. Which were both clearly visible beneath the sheer, shimmery dress she wore.

"Let's get a seat to watch the show," Reb said, putting his mouth next to my ear so I could hear him.

I nodded mutely. My brain was scrambling to put together all of the pieces I'd picked up over the last few weeks, and I couldn't quite manage words at the moment. Aside from processing the Dominatrix orchestrating a scene between the two men and herself, I was also coming to the realization that the 'club' Savannah had mentioned as the way Jace had met the guys was *this* club, Gilded Cage.

That should have freaked me out. *All* of this should have freaked me out. But, as Reb sat us down on a short loveseat, I was strangely *not* freaked out. In fact, I was feeling oddly hopeful. Coming here, being a part of this world, it seemed to bring the others together. The women had said they'd worked with the guys before moving into less-than-professional relationships, and I didn't doubt that this was a part of their lives now.

As Reb slid his arm around my waist and pulled me close, I let myself relax against his side and settled in to watch the show.

"ARE YOU OKAY?"

Reb's voice drew me out of my head where I'd been replaying the last few minutes at the club before we'd called it a night. The expression on the woman's face when she'd come that last time, her body held between the two men, both of them inside her, fighting to hold back their own orgasms until she found her release...it had been nothing short of ecstasy, and I couldn't help but wonder what it would be like to feel like that.

I nodded in answer to his question, not trusting myself to speak just yet.

"I didn't freak you out, bringing you tonight, did I?" He tucked some hair behind my ear, his tone concerned, his touch gentle.

I shook my head.

"Then talk to me, Paige."

I looked up at the name. "Just processing, that's all."

"Processing like you're trying to figure out the best way to quit working on my account without looking bad to your boss, or processing like you're trying to decide if you're even safe with me at all?"

I blinked, his question startling an honest answer out of

me. "Neither. Unless you want someone else working for you on this."

"I should." He sighed, then cupped the side of my face, his thumb brushing across the corner of my mouth. "Because work makes things...complicated."

After a moment, I asked, "Complicated as in you don't know how to break it to me you don't like the work I'm doing, or complicated as in there are *other* things you'd like us to be doing together?"

He slid his hand around to cup the back of my head. "Complicated as in I want you to come back to my place tonight."

My mind ran through all of the things I'd seen over the last few hours. Floggers. Some sort of electric wand thing. A strap-on. Handcuffs. Safe words. I had no doubt that going back to his place meant sex, and probably not the vanilla kind that most women experienced for their first time. I knew him well enough to know that he wouldn't pressure me into anything I wasn't willing to do, but if I did this, I didn't want it to become about him feeling like he had to worry about each step, especially since I knew he had misgivings about being my first.

All of this went through my head in a matter of seconds, probably because I'd already been thinking about it most of the night. This wasn't like before when I'd been shocked by the feel of him touching me, kissing me. Now, I knew what it was like to have his mouth and hands on me, and I knew that I wanted more.

I slid my hands across his chest and up his shoulders,

letting myself enjoy the way he felt. I rested my forearms on his shoulders and laced my fingers together behind his neck.

"I want that too."

THE BUTTERFLIES in my stomach were back again. After I'd admitted to Reb that I wanted to go with him, I'd expected things to get hot and heavy like they had before, but he'd surprised me with a single kiss. Granted, that kiss had been enough to make my panties even wetter than they already were, but there'd been no touching on his part. Me? I'd taken full advantage of the opportunity to explore as many muscles as I could.

Now, I was in his bedroom, watching him take off his shirt, and trying to pretend that my heart wasn't trying to jump out of my chest. He unbuttoned his pants but stopped short of removing them, instead, letting them hang low on his hips as he walked toward me.

His eyes locked with mine as he turned me around and moved my hair over my shoulder. He kissed the place where my shoulder met my neck, a gentle gesture that surprised me. Once the zipper was down, I let the dress fall to the floor before stepping out of it. My bra went next, and he wrapped his arms around me, fingers teasing across my nipples until they hardened. Then his hands dropped to my hips, and he lowered my panties until they, too, were on the floor.

"You're even more beautiful than I'd imagined," he said, breath hot against my ear. "And I've done quite a bit of imagining."

I turned around and took a small step back. I locked gazes and reached for his pants, each movement deliberate as I waited for some sort of command. It didn't come, though, so I went to my knees on my own. He uttered a low curse as I tugged his pants down his thighs, then dropped my eyes to focus on the long, thick shaft in front of me.

"You don't have to do this." His voice was rough, his entire body tense.

"Trust me," I said, licking my lips. "I want to."

I wrapped my hand around the base of him, holding him steady as I flicked my tongue across the tip of him, tasting the salt of sweat and pre-cum. He groaned as I began to lick him, long passes with the flat of my tongue from the very bottom to the top, swirling passes and teasing touches, each one getting him slippery enough so that I could begin to move my hand.

I'd never done this before, but I considered myself a fast learner. So, as I stroked him with firm, slow movements, I took the head of his cock into my mouth and let it slide over my tongue.

Now it was time to see how far I could go.

TWENTY-ONE
REB

She was going to kill me.

I was going to die with my cock being deep-throated by the sexiest virgin I'd ever seen, and all before I got the chance to show her just how good sex could be.

That thought was enough to prod me into action. I reached down and buried my hand in that thick, silky hair of hers, and with a reluctant groan, pulled her back. My cock slipped out of her mouth with an obscene, wet sound.

"Did I do something wrong?" Her voice was low, husky.

A part of me wondered what she would sound like if I took control and fucked her mouth, how long her voice would be rough from me using her the way a part of me wanted to.

"Not at all," I said, caressing her cheek. "But I don't want to come in your mouth." I traced her bottom lip with my thumb. "Not yet, anyway."

I took her hand, helped her to her feet, and then led her over to the bed. I opened my mouth, intending to tell her how I wanted her...and then I realized that I didn't know what to say.

Dammit! I was a Dom. Control and knowing what to do were part of who I was, but I didn't know how to be in control without being a Dom.

"Are you okay?" Paige asked, concern replacing the heat and lust I'd seen in her eyes just a few seconds ago.

I nodded, giving her a partial smile. "I'm just not sure how I want you."

"Don't overthink it."

She sat down on the edge of the mattress and pushed herself back until she was in the middle of the bed. She laid back on the pillows and parted her legs. As I watched, she slid her hand down her stomach. The heat in her eyes was back, as was the sexual tension in the room. Her fingers slipped over her pink, glistening skin, and then between her folds.

"Or should I just take care of things myself?"

I growled, and for a moment, I wanted to tell her that I was going to take her over my knee, because *no one* touched what was mine.

And she *was* mine.

But if I wanted her to be mine, and keep her mine, I couldn't risk scaring her away.

"You don't need to do that," I said as I crawled up on the bed. "Because I intend to take care of you." I hooked her legs over my shoulders and settled there. "Now, my Paige, move your hand."

She tasted just as good as she had that night in the limo and came just as fast, but I wasn't satisfied with giving her only one orgasm. I needed to make her come, needed to take her so high that she'd never want anyone else. I tightened my grip on her thighs and took her clit between my lips, sucking hard enough to roll her first climax into a second. She writhed as she moaned and gasped, her hands in my hair, and I worked on getting her to number three.

I would have been content to lay there for hours, but she began to pull at my hair, begging, "Please, Reb."

I moved up over her, high enough to keep my weight off of her, but low enough that her nipples were hard pebbles against my chest. She wrapped her legs around my waist, arched up against me. My cock was throbbing, aching, and the heat coming from her was almost too much to bear.

"Are you sure this is what you want?" I asked, brushing back her hair from her flushed face. "We can stop right now."

She reached up and grabbed the back of my neck, nails biting into my skin. "Don't you dare. I want you inside me."

I knew I should get up and retrieve a condom from my bedside table, but I hesitated. This was her first time, and even though it was selfish, I wanted something that made this more than just another fuck. I didn't know what we were to each other, or where we were going to go from here, but I did know that what I felt for her was nothing like what I'd felt in my past.

"Are you on the pill?"

Her eyes flew to mine, startled. A second later, they widened. "I am."

"May I...?"

I didn't finish the question before she answered, "Yes, please."

I kept my gaze on hers as I reached between us and positioned myself. "You tell me if I hurt you."

"Just go slow," she said with a nervous smile. "You're bigger than anything else I've had..." The flush on her cheeks deepened.

"I thought you said–"

"Virgin," she interrupted. "Yes. But that doesn't mean I haven't taken care of things myself."

Fuck. "Sometime soon, I'm going to want to see that." I slid the tip of my cock inside her, barely an inch but she still caught her breath.

"You want to watch me...ahh..." Another inch and she was already squeezing me like a vice.

"Hell, yes," I groaned. "I want to watch you fuck yourself with your fingers, with toys, but right now, Paige, I just want to fuck you."

Her legs tightened around me, and she raised her hips, taking me deeper in one smooth motion. "Then stop talking and do it."

I bent my head, kissing her hard and fast. "Yes, ma'am."

I drove the last couple inches into her and we both

cursed. She was hot and tight and perfect. I rocked against her, keeping some pressure and friction against her clit as I waited for her body to relax.

When she started to move underneath me, I reached down to cup her ass, then slid my hand to her thigh and pulled her leg higher. Skin against skin, we moved, neither one of us speaking. Usually, silence during sex freaked me out, but now, I found myself too preoccupied with studying all the nuances of her expressions, something new appearing with every stroke.

Pressure coiled low in my stomach, and I could feel my balls starting to tighten. I was almost there, but I needed her to get there first. I rose up on my knees, wrapping my arms around her waist to pull her up with me. Her mouth crashed into mine, and she ground down on me, our rhythm becoming jerky and uneven. It was nothing like the polished and smooth motions I'd had with others in the past, but this was somehow more real.

Her.

Me.

This.

I bit down on her bottom lip, and she cried out, her body seizing around mine. I cursed, clutching her close as I thrust up into her, my own orgasm taking my breath away. Her muscles contracted as I emptied myself inside her, and as pleasure coursed through me, my mind cleared of everything except her.

As we started to come down, I lowered us to the bed, keeping her in my arms even as my cock slid out of her.

Normally, I'd be rushing to get away, or freaking out since I was home and couldn't exactly go anywhere, but I was content where I was at the moment.

"I should go," she said after a couple minutes, breaking the silence blanketing us. "I mean, I can't–"

"Relax. It's okay. I've got you," I said as I kissed the top of her head. She relaxed back against me, and I tightened my arms around her.

I didn't know what the hell I was doing, but for the first time in a long time, my world had stopped spiraling, and I felt grounded.

I'D BEEN awake for the last twenty minutes, staring at the ceiling, but it wasn't because anything was wrong. All of the restless energy I'd had before was gone, and so was the depression. I didn't want a drink. I was quite fine with lying here, hands folded under my head, thinking about my night with Paige. She'd left this morning, but we'd spent the night together, which was a first for me.

This morning hadn't been nearly as awkward as I'd thought, though there'd been plenty of half-sentences and pregnant pauses.

Pregnant.

Shit.

She said she was on the pill, and I believed her, but nothing besides abstinence was one hundred percent. Sine and Alix were proof of that. I hadn't been as shocked by his acceptance of the situation as Jace had been, but at the time, I'd thought how glad I was that I wasn't in his position.

Except now, I was thinking about what would happen if I *was* in that position...and it actually didn't sound that bad. Not that I wanted Paige to get pregnant. Certainly not right now. But the idea of having a baby, of *her* having *my* baby–

My phone rang, the ringtone telling me that it wasn't the person I wanted to talk to, but I still had to answer it.

"Hey, Chester."

"Be at my office in forty minutes."

"What–"

He'd already hung up. I rolled my eyes and tossed the phone onto the table. At least he gave me time to take a shower.

When I walked into his office forty-five minutes later, Chester was all smiles which, considering the state of his teeth, wasn't really a good thing. It also made me wary, because when he smiled like that, it usually meant he was up to something.

"What was so urgent?" I asked.

He motioned for me to follow him, and I sighed. There was no talking to him when he got some idea in his head. He wasn't the best manager in the world, and I'd always been able to afford better, but Chester was the one who'd found me messing around on a guitar in a college coffee house and offered to negotiate my first contract. He'd never cheated me that I knew of, and he'd always fought to get me the things that were important to me. We weren't friends, and most of the time I didn't really even like him, but he'd done right by me professionally.

Especially when it came to hiring Paige.

I owed him a lot more than my musical career now.

"Is everything okay?" I asked, not liking the vibe I sensed in the air.

"Everything's great," he said as he moved to his desk, but his eyes were twitchy, a faint sheen of sweat on his forehead making me wonder if he was on the verge of a heart attack.

"Then why—"

A giggle came from behind me, and I turned slowly to find a blonde on the couch. Not just any blonde. Her.

Mitzi was only twenty-three, but she'd aged nearly a decade since I'd last seen her. She'd streaked her hair with hot pink, replacing the purple she'd had before that, but her attempt to look like a teenager made her look more desperate than anything else. She'd lost so much weight over the past couple months, and she'd always been thin to begin with. Her skin was leathery, wrinkled and sagging.

And the moment I saw the table in front of her, I knew why. Bottles of alcohol, some empty, some not. Rolled joints. Cigarettes half-smoked. White powder. Needles and rubber tubing.

She smiled up at me. "Hey, baby."

I was frozen in shock.

I'd known about some of it. The pot and the alcohol. I knew she'd smoked too, but I hadn't let her do it around me. I hadn't known about the harder stuff though. If I had, I would've tried to get her help.

I shook my head, breaking the grip of surprise that had held me. "What are you doing here, Mitzi?" Seeing her didn't hurt anymore. Hell, it hadn't actually hurt in a while. Even when it happened, it'd been more humiliating than painful, especially after she'd blamed me.

"Chester and I were just talking about old times." She leaned forward and rubbed her finger across the powder residue, then rubbed it on her gums. "All the fun we had."

My feelings for Mitzi were gone, even the negative ones, but I liked to think I was still a good person. A decent guy who couldn't sit by and watch someone destroy herself.

I crouched down to put myself on her level but didn't touch her. I couldn't bring myself to do that. "I'd like to help you, if you'll let me."

She let out a shrill laugh, rocking back so hard that one shoulder of her shirt slipped off, dropping low enough for me to see the top of her nipple. "I don't need your help."

"Come on, Reb, I've got some fine whiskey calling our names. We need to sit down and talk."

I straightened, glaring at Chester. "What the hell? You're the one who forced a public relations rep on me because I was drinking too much, and now you're offering me a drink? And what the fuck's with all that shit?" I waved my hand at the table.

He gave me a sour grin. "That's me taking care of your business."

"*My* business?" I could feel Mitzi's eyes on me, but I said what I needed to say. "She and I ended things months ago. She's not my business anymore. But she still doesn't need to be using any of that shit... especially with you! What the fuck, Chester?"

He shrugged, seemingly unaffected by my anger and my accusations. "She's a grown-up." He poured two drinks and held out one to me while he started drinking the other.

I glared at him. I knew I should leave, but I also knew I couldn't leave things like this. This was my fucking manager, and I needed to understand why he was doing this.

"I'll just have some water." I moved to the small fridge he kept over on the counter and got myself a bottle of water and twisted off the lid.

"Suit yourself," he said with another shrug. "I didn't have a problem with you drinking."

I stared at him, the bottle frozen just inches from my mouth. "What?"

He rolled his eyes. What had happened the Chester I knew? I looked around the room, searching for hidden cameras. Was I being punked?

He waved a hand at me. "You said I hired that girl because I had a problem with you drinking, but that's not why. You did some stupid shit, and we needed things to cool down. She seemed like a good way to get that done quick."

I shook my head. Out of the corner of my eye, I saw Mitzi pick up one of the joints and light it. The sickly-sweet smell joined the rest of the scents in the office, and I was tempted to take back the whiskey just to get my mind on something else.

"Now that she's done her job," Chester continued, "you can knock off the charity shit."

I could only stare at him. "Excuse me?"

Mitzi let out a cackle, and another puff of smoke came with it. "You look like a pucking fussy." She frowned. "Nope. That's not it."

"The label's gonna think you went soft." Chester poured himself another drink. "If you were some pussy pop star, that might fly, but you've got an image to protect. Two weekends are enough."

I remembered what Paige said about why she hadn't just given me the first community service project she could find. Basically, that it was the difference between paying a penance and actually changing how people saw me. She saw me as a good man, and I wanted others to see me that way too.

"Reb." Mitzi grabbed my arm. "You really gotta try this shit. It's amazing."

Her pupils were so wide that I could barely see any color at all.

I jerked my arm away. "You need to stop that shit."

She stuck out her bottom lip. "Why're you always so mean?"

It was the sort of thing a spoiled child would say, but all it made me think of was how she'd said me being 'mean' had been the reason she'd cheated. And that hadn't been the least of the accusations she'd thrown my way.

Surely I was being punked, or could two people I thought I knew have changed so drastically? Or had I just been to stupid or self-absorbed to see it?

I set my bottle of water down on the table. "I need to take a piss. Get your head on straight, Chester, and then we can talk about how things are going to be from here on out."

TWENTY-TWO
PAIGE

With my limited knowledge, when a woman lost her virginity in a toe-curling experience with a drop-dead gorgeous rock god, she tended to tell someone. Her best friend usually. Maybe her mom. But I couldn't tell anyone. Even if I'd had someone I considered a close enough friend in whom I could confide something like this, I still wouldn't do it. Not while I was working with Reb.

Which meant I had no one to help me sort through all of the thoughts crowding my mind.

"Paige, can you come here?" Sybil called from her office.

I hurried inside but didn't bother taking a seat. No matter how polite her question, she wasn't asking me to have a conversation. She wanted to tell me to do something.

"I can't get ahold of Chester Lhaw. His check bounced, and Mr. Dwight wants you to go talk to him about it."

I frowned. "Re..." I cleared my throat, blinking rapidly to clear my confusion. "Mr. Union's check bounced?" That didn't sound right. "Shouldn't I talk to him directly? I haven't really had much contact with Mr. Lhaw, but I don't think he handles Mr. Union's money."

Actually, I knew he didn't. Something here wasn't adding up.

Sybil gave me a sharp look. "Just do as you're told and get back here with a new check."

I was tempted to point out that I doubted upper management had specifically requested I personally go get a check. As far as I was aware, Mr. Dwight didn't even know my name. But, then, I'd been suspicious for a while that Sybil had been pawning off some of her work on me. I didn't mind, not when I knew I could count on satisfied clients to be honest about who'd actually done the work.

"Of course."

I took a taxi to Chester's office and thanked the driver when he expressed concern over dropping me off there. I had to admit, I was more than a little surprised to learn that Reb's manager had an office in that part of town. I would've expected something much bigger and definitely in a better neighborhood. Then again, I'd already learned that Reb wasn't really like anything I'd expected. For all I knew, his manager had an office at that location so that he could find talent others might overlook.

The minute I stepped inside, however, I began to rethink my theory. I wrinkled my nose and hoped I wouldn't end up with a contact high. The entire place reeked of marijuana, alcohol, and body odor. What I knew of Reb didn't mesh with where I found myself. The place wasn't dirty, but it wasn't exactly clean either. Plastic plants sat at random intervals, even their leaves managing to look wilted. The desk was cluttered, the computer ancient.

"Hello?" I coughed, then tried again when no one answered, "Hello? Mr. Lhaw?"

"Back here."

A gravelly voice drifted out of the half-open door I could see from where I stood, but I couldn't see anything else, including the owner of the voice. I didn't particularly like the idea of going back there on my own, and everything I'd ever been told about how to be smart as a woman in the city alone told me this was a bad idea. Still, I doubted Sybil would accept an excuse for not doing what I'd been told to do.

I took out my phone, tapped out a quick message to Reb, letting him know I was at his agent's office, and then held my thumb over *send* as I walked through the door and into a smoke-clouded room.

It took me nearly half a minute for my eyes to adjust, and when they did, I wished they hadn't.

Reb was there. Sprawled on a couch that looked like its better days had been some time in the mid-seventies, his eyes bleary and unfocused, his face slack. His shirt was half-off, one sleeve still around his wrist. He didn't even seem to see me, but that could have been because he was clearly high on whatever he'd been snorting or shooting...or it could have been due to the half-naked woman squirming on his lap.

Half-naked was being generous. Her shirt hung over the back of the couch, and if she'd been wearing a bra, it was nowhere currently to be seen. Her breasts were small, her nipples pierced, and I could make out a tattoo, though not what it said. She had on a pair of hot-pink stilettos to match her hair and a leather mini-skirt that was pushed up high enough on her hips that I could see a hot pink thong.

I recognized her too. Mitzi Adler. Reb's so-called ex-girlfriend. The one he'd told me he'd caught in bed with two other men. The one who'd sent him into a downward spiral so bad that he'd needed me to fix it.

She tossed her hair back over her shoulder, only now seeming to realize that she had an audience. She winked at me and went back to grinding on Reb. She started kissing his neck, her hand moving down between them...

I looked away. I couldn't watch anymore, but I refused to leave before I did what I'd come here to do. I wouldn't cry or even acknowledge that I felt anything at all about what was going on. I was a professional, even though my heart was pounding so hard in my chest I almost couldn't breathe.

"Who're you?" With his greasy hair and beady eyes, Chester looked like the stereotypical sleazy manager portrayed in movies and on TV.

I took a deep breath and pretended not to notice that his hand was in his pants and got right to the point. I didn't want to be there any longer than absolutely necessary.

Emotions roiled inside of me...anger and disappointment, and something else. A deep, deep sadness that threatened to spill from my eyes and down my cheeks.

"I'm Paige Ryce, and I work for the PR firm you hired on behalf of Mr. Union. Sybil Feldt sent me regarding your payment." I ignored his greedy gaze running all over my body and wondered if I'd be able to run home for a shower before going back to work. "We need you to write another check as it seems this last one bounced. Some sort of misunderstanding, we're sure, but we do need that payment again."

Chester stared at me for a few seconds, his hand moving in a motion that left no doubt about what he was doing. I was just thankful he hadn't whipped his cock out. Yet.

"I don't have my checkbook here," he said finally. "You want to come back to my place, and I'll get it for you?"

"No, that's all right." How I managed not to gag, I didn't know. "We'll have a courier stop by first thing tomorrow to pick it up."

Sybil had told me to get the check, but there was no way in hell I'd be going back to this asshole's place for it. That was where I drew the line. If Sybil pushed it, I'd threaten to go to Mr. Dwight about all of her work I'd been doing.

"Want some blow?"

My nails bit into my palms. "Pardon me?"

Chester leered at me. "I got some great stuff. Loosen you right up. You can join us."

I turned on my heel and walked away, taking the time only to toss a few words over my shoulder. "First thing tomorrow, Mr. Lhaw, we're going to want that check."

And then I was outside in the crisp September air, trying to remember that I couldn't cry here. This was all my fault. Not what Reb was doing. That was his own stupid mistake. No, what was my fault was the pain in my heart. I'd known better than to get involved with him. He was a client *and* a musician. Two things I'd sworn I'd stay away from.

And that meant I wasn't going to cry over him. I didn't deserve that luxury. Instead, I'd do what I should have been doing all along and work my ass off.

No more repeating my mother's mistakes.

TWENTY-THREE
REB

I woke up about three seconds before I lurched forward and vomited on a rug that had seen better days.

A rug that I didn't recognize.

Where was I, and why did I feel like I had cotton stuffed in my head?

"Hey there, sexy sleepy."

I knew that voice, and it wasn't one I wanted to hear. "Mitzi?"

As the haze cleared, the memories of earlier today started to come back. Coming to see Chester. Mitzi being here. The drugs. The alcohol.

But I hadn't taken anything, so why did I feel like I'd spent the last few hours partying?

"What the hell happened today?" I frowned, searching through the haze of my memory. "It is still today, right?"

She shrugged and took a puff on a half-burnt joint. "No clue."

I pushed up from the couch and immediately grabbed the arm as a wave of dizziness washed over me. "What...fuck..."

"You need to loosen up." She threw a cigarette butt at me.

I ignored her. My stomach was still rolling a bit, and my head was starting to hurt. My mouth tasted like...well, like puke.

I reached for my bottle of water. There was barely a mouthful left, but it'd be enough to rinse out my mouth before I grabbed another one. I tossed the cap onto the table and had the bottle halfway to my mouth when I stopped. Mitzi was watching me, her attention locked in on my hand.

The hand holding my bottle of water.

The water that I'd left on the table when I'd gone to the bathroom earlier.

I hadn't gotten there before, but I was there now. I lowered my hand. "Did you put something in my water?"

She gave me a guilty little smirk I recognized from when we were together. "Chester did it."

I looked around. "Where is he?"

"Not here." She stretched lazily, her shirt riding up to show her flat stomach.

A vague memory of that stomach, of bare breasts, drifted across my mind. Why? I hadn't seen her naked since that night when I'd caught her being double-teamed by two overweight, sweaty bastards with bad hygiene.

"What the hell did you give me?" I tossed the bottle

toward the overflowing trash can, ignoring it when it missed.

"Not me," she insisted. "Chester."

"I don't give a fuck who actually drugged me! What was it?!"

"Just some Valium." She scowled at me. "Because you needed to chill out."

I stumbled into the bathroom and splashed some water on my face, then found some mouthwash and used the rest of the bottle to at least fix that problem. When I made my way back out, Mitzi had stripped down to her thong and was dancing on the couch.

"I'm out of blow," she announced in a sing-song voice that pounded on my last nerve. "Go get me more."

I stared at her for a moment, but not because she was almost naked. It was like I was seeing her for the first time. "You need to get some help, Mitzi. Living like this is going to kill you."

"Pfft." She flapped her hands at me. "Go get me blow and I'll blow you." She cackled, clearly pleased with herself. "No one else'll be doing it now. Not after the story comes out."

I frowned at her. "What story?"

She bounced off the couch and came to stand in front of me. "The one Chester's selling to make you look like less of a pussy."

"What are you talking..."

More memories came forward. Memories of Mitzi on my lap. Touching me. Kissing me. The taste of pot and tobacco on my lips. Then, something else. Something I couldn't quite remember but had a feeling was important.

"He got lots of good pictures and even some video for TV news. We're gonna be headlines."

I tried to process her words, tried to make sense of why the manager I'd trusted for so long would set me up like this. No understanding dawned.

"Why the hell would he do that? I'm supposed to be getting *good* press now."

She rolled her eyes. "Sex, drugs, and rock 'n roll. People just wanna see their stars do some penance, and public flogging isn't really a thing." She sneered at me. "Wouldn't surprise me if you were into that though."

I suddenly felt sick again, but this time it wasn't anything physical. "Did we–?"

I couldn't finish the question, and even though I knew I *needed* to know the answer, I wasn't sure I *wanted* to know.

She gave me a coy look. "You could watch the video."

She was right. I could find all of the answers I needed by getting to Chester before he imploded things.

"Or you could ask that prude bitch of yours."

I stopped mid-step, the last piece of the puzzle falling into place. No, no, that wasn't...I closed my eyes. Very slowly, I turned back to her, needing confirmation to what I already knew. "Explain."

SHIT, shit, shit, shit...

The professional part of me had wanted to go straight for Chester, stop him from taking things public, but it had been barely a moment's consideration. Everything else in me had been screaming to get to Paige and set things straight. What she thought about me meant more than anyone else's opinion. I needed her to know that whatever she'd seen, it hadn't been me. I hadn't chosen to do any of it.

It was late enough that I went straight to her apartment and prayed that she'd agree to talk to me.

"Paige, it's me. Please let me come up. We need to talk."

She buzzed me in without a word, but at least she hadn't ignored me. When I got to her door, I knocked and braced myself. After a moment, I heard the locks turning, and then the door opened.

"Come in."

Any hope I'd felt disappeared at the ice in her words.

I glanced at her as I walked past. She was in a pair of loose flannel pants and a camisole, her hair wet and braided. And her face was completely blank. I scrubbed my hand over my chin, and then up into my hair, scowling at the feel of it.

I didn't even want to think about what had been on that couch.

"Everything you think I did, I didn't do," I blurted out, unable to figure out any other way to approach the subject.

Her jaw tightened, as did her spine. I could feel her anger and revulsion radiating off her in waves. "Staying clean and sober was part of our deal. I can't do my job if you don't do what I ask. I'll meet with Sybil tomorrow to move your account over to her, and she can handle things from there."

"I don't want anyone else working with me," I said. Then I shook my head. "You know what, I don't care about any of that. I just care about you knowing that I didn't do what–"

"I heard you," she snapped, her eyes still angry and something else...wounded. "But I know what I saw."

"But you don't know what happened before that."

She raised an eyebrow as she folded her arms. "I saw the booze and the joints and all the rest of that shit. And I saw your girlfriend grinding on you with her tits hanging out. Doesn't take a genius to figure it out."

Okay, not so cold anymore. She was pissed, but I preferred that to the possibility that she didn't feel anything for me at all.

"I swear to you, Paige, it wasn't what it looked like."

She shook her head. "It doesn't matter."

Something in me snapped. I moved toward her, backing her against the door. "Like hell it doesn't."

And then I kissed her.

TWENTY-FOUR
PAIGE

He'd backed me into a corner, almost literally, to steal a kiss, but for a few blissful moments, all I could do was grab the front of his shirt and pull him closer. My head and heart told me I was being stupid, but my body didn't care. It craved his touch like some sort of drug.

And that was the thought that finally broke through, giving me the strength I needed to push him away.

"You can't do that." I glared at him and tried to pretend that my hands weren't shaking. "You can't come in here and act like a kiss is going to make me forget what you did."

The muscle in his jaw popped, and he looked at me intently. "What you saw and what I did are two different things."

I wanted to believe him, wanted to believe that the real him was the man I'd seen with those kids and with the veterans. The man who, contrary to everything I'd ever believed, I'd slept with.

"I might've been a virgin until recently, but I've never been naïve." I started to put my hands in my pockets and then remembered that these pants didn't have any. "I know how guys like you think. It's sex, drugs, and rock 'n roll, right?"

"Paige–"

"And don't try to tell me that you're different," I interrupted before he could say anything sweet or charming. "My mother spent more than six years on the road with one rock band or another, some big names, some not. And she fucked a lot of them. But that's all it was. Never anything more. They didn't treat her badly, but when she got pregnant with me, she didn't even think about trying to figure out who the father was. She knew that, no matter who he was, he wasn't responsible enough to take care of a kid, even if he wanted to be involved, and she wasn't going to subject me to that."

"That's not fair, Paige, and you know it." His eyes flashed. "You can't hold me responsible for things other people did more than twenty years ago."

"I'm not," I snapped. "I'm just saying that I know how musicians like you are. You drink, and you fuck around, and you trash hotel rooms and do drugs–"

"I don't do drugs," he said through gritted teeth. "And yes, I did those other things, but that's in the past."

"A few hours ago isn't far enough in the past to be using it that way."

He shook his head, the anger on his face changing to

desperation. "Will you just listen to me? Hear me out? Please."

I clenched my jaw and nodded once. I'd listen to him, and then I'd tell him to leave.

"Chester called me and asked me to come over so we could talk about some business stuff," Reb said. The words began pouring out of him. "When I got there, Mitzi was there, and all sorts of shit was there too. She was using, and Chester asked me if I wanted a drink, but I said no. I got a bottle of water, and when I went to the bathroom, I left it on the table. I didn't think they'd do anything to it."

I held up a hand. "Are you saying they roofied you?"

He shrugged. "I guess you could say that. Everything after that is fuzzy or completely blank. I only know you were there because when I woke up, Mitzi told me. She said that they'd given me some Valium."

"Why would they do that?"

"She said Chester has some half-assed idea that people are going to think I'm going soft if you clean up my image too much, but I think he's doing it because he knows I'm getting sick of his shit and he thinks he can use the story to make it so another manager wouldn't want to take me on."

What he was saying made a sort of sense, but I latched onto one word more than others. "What story?"

Reb flushed with anger and embarrassment, and ran all ten fingers through his hair. "He took pictures and video that makes it look like I was...well, that I was doing what you thought I was doing. He's out selling it now." He started to reach for me, then stopped himself. "Wait...can I ask why you were even in his office?"

Damn, the check. "My company received a bounced check for our services, and I was sent to get another one."

He gaped at me, shaking his head. "My check bounced?" He ran another hand through his hair, this time pulling at the roots. "That can't be possible...unless... dammit! Chester!"

I watched his face morph through a variety of emotions and he attempted to process all that his manager may or may not have done. "I'm sorry."

He shook his head again and met my eyes. "All of that can wait. What I want you to know is that I could have gone after Chester to stop him from publishing those lies. I want you, Paige, more than I've wanted anything in a long time. You're what matters to me."

I shook my head. "I believe you, but wanting me isn't enough for me to think this is a good idea. I shouldn't have let anything happen in the first place."

I believed what I was saying, but I wasn't telling him the whole truth. I didn't tell him how much it had hurt me to see him like that, and how I knew I needed to get out now before I got in too deep. I wasn't sure I'd be able to survive having my heart broken by him when he inevitably moved on. Because him staying with me wasn't something I could imagine. Not when he was keeping a part of himself from me.

"You need to go." I couldn't look at him.

"Please, Paige." He moved closer, but I still didn't raise

my head. "Give me a chance to prove to you that I'm different. If I can't, then I'll leave, and I'll never bother you again."

I didn't want him to go. I wanted to try, to see if we could make things work. But if I was going to take a risk, he needed to do the same.

TWENTY-FIVE
REB

She wasn't looking at me, and she hadn't answered me yet, but she also hadn't kicked me out...or kicked me in the nuts, either. She said she believed me, which meant she was hesitating either because she really thought I was going to treat her the way those men had treated her mother. Or she didn't want me the way I wanted her, and this was her way of trying to get out of having to tell me.

My confidence had been thrown by what happened with Mitzi, but my night with Paige had shown me that the electricity between us was real. I wasn't imagining this connection. I just needed to get her to acknowledge it.

I took a step toward her, the downcast eyes and down-turned head speaking to every one of my instincts as a Dom.

"Look at me."

I hadn't heard that command in my voice in a while, and a part of me worried that it'd make her balk. Instead, she raised her head. Her eyes were wide, and when her lips parted, I couldn't stop myself from leaning down to kiss her again.

Only to find myself stopped by a hand on my chest.

"You stink."

The blunt statement startled a laugh out of me. "What?"

"You stink," she repeated, giving me a stern look. "If you want to get near me ever again, you need to clean up."

I grinned, some of the tension easing. She wasn't saying no. "Are you offering me the use of your shower?"

The saucy turn of her lips sent the blood rushing to my cock.

"If you don't mind smelling like me."

I took a step back because it was either that or drag her into the shower with me, which I was still trying to tell myself was a bad idea. Her shower wasn't nearly big enough for the things I wanted to do to her.

"Promise you'll be here when I get out." I didn't make it a request, and it felt so damn good to be giving orders again. So much so that I added another one. "Naked."

A strange expression crossed her face, like she was coming to a decision on something. I only hoped it was a good one.

"I'll give you a chance to prove you're different," she said, "but only if you're honest about what you want."

I frowned. "What are you talking about?"

"I can't be with someone who feels like they have to hide who they are." Her voice was firm, but not harsh. "I don't mean you have to take out a billboard or something, but if you really want to have a relationship with me, you have to be honest about who you are and what you want."

"I–" My mouth snapped closed. A sick feeling settled in my stomach. "I don't *need* it."

She gave me a soft smile. "You want to know why it was so easy for me to believe that you were the same as all the men my mom had warned me about?"

"Because I'm a pervert." I repeated Mitzi's accusation with all the bitterness I felt. "Not really a news flash, Paige."

"No."

I blinked at the force she put into that single word.

"I went to that club with you, and I never once said anything there was perverted about what I saw. Different, yes. Shocking, okay, I'll give you that. But why would you think I'd..." She gave me a hard look. "Is that why things were so...*vanilla* when we had sex?"

The knot in my stomach tightened. "I thought it was good for you. I mean, you came...right?"

She put her hand on my arm. "Yes, Reb. It was better than I'd ever thought my first time would be. I'm not complaining. I'm just saying that after the things I saw at Gilded Cage, I really thought you would've wanted to do... you know..." A blush stained her cheeks.

I shook my head, hands curling into fists. "No. I learned what happens when I force my...preferences on someone. I won't do that to you."

She stared at me for a moment, then her eyes narrowed. "That bitch."

Okay, not what I expected.

"That's what *Mitzi* said you did to her."

Paige was furious, but not with me.

"I know you, Reb, and you'd never force yourself on someone. If she would've said no, you would've listened."

"Of course I would've listened."

"She's full of shit," Paige insisted. Her expression became sly. "Besides, how am I going to learn if you won't teach me?"

"*Teach* you?"

She nodded, heat smoldering in her eyes. "I'm willing to risk it if you are, but you have to put it all on the line too."

TWENTY-SIX
PAIGE

My stomach was in knots and I didn't know what to do with my hands. Reb had been in my shower for ten minutes, and I doubted he'd be much longer. At least, I hoped he wouldn't be. I was starting to have doubts about my decision. Not the one to give Reb a second chance, but the one where I was going to have sex with him when he got out of the shower.

Kinky sex.

Romance wasn't my favorite genre, but I'd read a few over the years, including some that had a little S&M in them. Reading about it, however, and actually doing it were two completely different things. Hell, *seeing* it live and doing it myself were worlds apart.

"I thought I gave you clear instructions about how you were supposed to wait for me."

I froze. I'd been so caught up in my thoughts that I hadn't heard the shower stop or the bathroom door open, and now, my brain was scrambling to make sense of what Reb was saying.

"Turn around, Paige."

It was a command, not a request, but the sort of demand I heard wasn't some sort of misogynistic power-trip. I'd heard that same authoritative note in the woman's voice at Gilded Cage when she'd ordered her men around. It was the voice of a Dominant, regardless of gender.

I turned to face him, heat flooding my body as I saw he wore only a towel around his waist. I wasn't so noble that I didn't feel a thrill at the realization that this gorgeous man wanted *me*.

"Did I, or did I not, say that I wanted you *naked* when I got out of the shower?"

The unadulterated desire shining in his eyes made my mouth dry and my pussy wet.

"Paige." My name was a warning.

"Yes." The word was little more than a whisper. I cleared my throat and tried again. "Yes, you did."

"Then why aren't you naked?"

The question was casual, almost as if he'd been asking why I didn't have an umbrella when it was raining. Then he tossed his towel toward my hamper and, even though I'd seen him naked before, I completely lost the ability to think clearly.

I suddenly became aware that Reb was talking to me. I jerked my head up, cheeks flaming.

"I suppose I'll give you a pass for not listening that

time," he said with an amused smile. "But you still haven't done as you were told."

I kept my eyes on him as I pulled my shirt over my head. I folded it and put it on the dresser, then took off my pants and did the same.

"Good girl." He didn't look away as he walked toward me, his hand dropping to his cock. "Now, face the bed and bend over."

"What?"

He stopped less than a foot away from me. "You said you wanted me to be honest about the things that I want."

I nodded. "I do."

He reached out and took a lock of hair between his fingers. "You know a bit about BDSM. Do you know what happens when a sub disobeys their Dom?"

I shivered, but it wasn't an unpleasant sensation. "They get punished."

He nodded. "They get punished. And I'm a Dom, Paige. What does that make you?"

I understood now what he was doing. Part of this was sexual, but part of it was making sure that I truly knew what I was getting into.

"I'm the sub."

He moved a few inches closer, and I could smell my shampoo and soap. It smelled better on him.

"Whose sub, Paige? Whose sub are you?"

I swallowed hard. "Yours."

He leaned down and brushed his lips across mine. "And what did you do?"

The words came easier than I'd expected. "I disobeyed."

He nodded. "Yes, you did." After a pause, he added, "What should I do about that?"

My mind immediately flashed back to what I'd seen at the club. If I gave the answer I knew he wanted, I didn't know exactly what he was going to do, and the possibilities weren't equally appealing. Which meant I needed to trust him.

"Punish me," I whispered.

For a moment, he stared at me, as if he couldn't believe I'd actually said it, and then he pulled me to him, skin against skin as our mouths crashed together. I moaned as he ravaged my mouth, his fingers digging into the small of my back, into my neck. I thought I'd known how powerful he was before, but it was nothing compared to the strength I felt in his body now.

By the time he finally broke the kiss, it was all I could do not to jump him right then and there. My entire body ached. His cock was hard and hot against my stomach, leaving a trail of pre-cum on my skin as he moved a few inches back. His eyes dropped, and he used his thumb to rub the salty liquid into my skin.

"I like the idea of you wearing my cum." His hand moved up to my breast, and he squeezed hard enough to make me catch my breath, but not quite hard enough to actually hurt. "But not tonight."

He took a full step back and raised an eyebrow. I almost asked him what he wanted, but then I remembered.

I turned around, took a slow breath, and then bent over. I placed my hands flat on the blanket...and waited.

"Each Dom has their own way of doling out punishments," he said. "Even my friends and I don't come at things the same way."

He was staying just out of my line of sight, and I had no doubt he was doing it intentionally. Using anticipation to ramp up the tension.

"I believe in punishments growing in time and intensity, so for this first offense, I'll be using my hand."

I flinched as he touched me, but his palm only rested against the top of my ass.

"You need a safe word."

His tone had changed, and I immediately felt guilty for flinching. "I'm sorry."

"That's usually not a good safe word."

"For flinching," I clarified. "It wasn't fear, just nerves." I risked a look over my shoulder. "I trust you."

The tension on his face eased. "Thank you."

"Bananas."

He gave me a puzzled look.

"My safe word. Bananas."

He nodded, amusement dancing in his eyes. "All right then. Let's begin."

I nodded and faced front again. The next time his hand came down, it wasn't a touch. His palm hit my ass with a cracking sound, and I gasped. More blows came, one right after the other, alternating from one side to the other until my ass was burning. The pain wasn't unbearable, more like a sunburn sort of sensitivity and sting, but it was definitely intense.

"All done." His voice was almost gentle as he ran his hand up my spine. "Now, my Paige, what will you do when I give you an order?"

"Obey." I closed my eyes and concentrated on his touch. The heat of his hand, so different from the more pleasant feeling a little farther south.

"Good answer." His hands settled on my hips, thumbs stroking my skin. "I didn't bring any condoms with me tonight."

This was about more than him just checking to make sure I was okay with us not using a condom. This was about whether or not I really did trust him. If I thought he was lying and he'd had sex with Mitzi, I wouldn't want him inside me bare.

"I don't want anything between us...fuck!" The curse burst out of me as he buried himself deep with one stroke. I wasn't even close to use to this, but I sure as hell didn't want him to stop.

He wound his hand in my hair, using it to leverage me as he drove into me with one thrust after another. Each one drove another cry from my lips even as the air escaped my lungs. I curled my fingers into fists, the comforter keeping my nails from my palms.

"I'm going to fuck you in front of a mirror sometime," Reb broke the silence. "I want to see every expression on your face when I take you from behind."

His free hand moved underneath me, pinching my

nipple between finger and thumb hard enough to send a jolt of pain through me. He held on to my sensitive flesh, even as my breasts moved with the force of his thrusts, causing new little ripples of pain with each stroke.

"I love these tits. Perfect nipples for clamps." His hand moved down between my legs, fingers finding my clit. "We'll try those out before we move on to putting one on this pretty little thing."

I whimpered at the thought of something pinching my clit as hard as he was holding my nipple. But I wanted it. Him spanking me had turned me on more than I'd realized, and I knew he could show me things that I'd never find with anyone else. Because I'd never let anyone else this close.

"I'm going to fuck your ass one day." He spoke so matter-of-factly that it took a moment for his words to sink in. "And then we're going to try some double penetration." Before I could react, he leaned over and put his mouth against my ear. "Don't worry, my Paige. I don't plan on ever sharing you with anyone. But there are ways to have just as much fun."

I groaned as he bit down on my shoulder, then shouted his name as he pressed his fingers hard against my clit, forcing me over the edge. My arms shook, elbows giving out as an orgasm ripped through me. I yelped as his grip on my hair tightened, holding me in place as he slammed into me one more time.

As he came, he said only two words.

"Thank you."

TWENTY-SEVEN
REB

I'd dozed a bit after I'd cleaned us up and put us to bed. I'd always taken good care of the subs I'd fucked, but I hadn't literally gone to bed with them. I hadn't wanted to give them the wrong impression. Occasionally, I'd fallen asleep after sex, but Mitzi had been the only other woman I'd ever consciously chosen to go to sleep with, and only then occasionally. Those nights, I'd hardly been able to rest, constantly aware of her presence, and not in a good way. It had been uncomfortable, something to endure rather than enjoy.

Waking up with Paige in my arms again wasn't like that at all.

She was curled into me, her back against my chest. We were both still naked, and I was hyperaware of all the places where our skin touched. Being with her was so different than being with anyone else. Not because she was inexperienced. She looked past my image to see me, rather than looking past me to see my image, and now, knowing the sort of baggage she had when it came to guys like me, I was even more impressed.

Now, as I brushed some hair back from her face, I allowed myself to acknowledge that what I felt for her was much deeper than *wanting*, more selfless than *needing*. I was falling in love with her.

The thought should have terrified me. I'd never said that to any woman who wasn't family. Not really. I'd said 'love ya' and 'right back at you' to Mitzi a few times near the end when she'd been saying it to me almost every day, but I'd never flat out said 'I love you' or 'I'm falling in love with you' to her. *Want* had been the word I'd used when it came to my feelings for her.

The bedroom was dark, leaving Paige's features in shadows, but I didn't need light to see her. I knew her face and body as well as my own.

I kissed her shoulder and pulled the blankets more snuggly around us both. I was tempted to use my fingers and tongue to wake her, then slip into her from behind and take her nice and slow. My stomach clenched at the thought, and my interested cock when from half-hard to uncomfortable.

No. I couldn't do that to her. I'd been rough earlier, and while I didn't doubt that she would've told me to stop if she hadn't enjoyed herself, she was still new to all of this and needed time to recover.

I needed to remember to talk to her about how the Dom / sub relationship worked outside of the obvious bedroom interactions. I didn't want her to think that I expected her to be submissive all the time. Hell, I liked when she pushed me. I had enough people kissing my ass. I needed someone like her to keep me in check out there. Some things, though, would remain the same. I wasn't the sort of Dom who insisted on controlling every aspect of her life, telling her when and what to eat, what to wear, who she could spend time with, but I did take my responsibility to care for her seriously.

Which meant she had to be honest with me if I was too rough or if she needed a break. I'd always push her limits, test her comfort zones, but I'd never hurt her. Despite what most people thought of my world, a sub's well-being was a Dom's top priority.

When I couldn't ignore the call of nature any longer, I eased myself out of bed. My clothes from earlier today were hanging in the bathroom, still damp from my attempts to wash at least some of the smell from them, but since I didn't have any other clothes, I pulled my jeans back on, grimacing at the cold fabric. Still, it was better than wandering around Paige's apartment naked. At least they finally smelled better.

As much as I enjoyed sleeping next to Paige, I was too restless to get back into bed. It wasn't the normal restlessness I got after sex. I didn't have any urge to leave, but something had me on edge. It was a familiar feeling, but I couldn't quite place it yet.

I went into her kitchen and got myself a bottle of water, then paced around the small space, taking in all the details I'd missed before. Sparse furniture, and none of it looked brand-new, but they weren't the ragtag furnishings I'd expected from a recent college graduate. They matched relatively well and looked like they'd been taken care of. She had a small television in the corner, but the stack of books next to a large overstuffed armchair suggested she spent more time reading than watching TV.

Everything was neat and orderly, which didn't surprise me. Paige struck me as a person who wanted things in her place but wasn't so obsessive about it that that place didn't look lived in.

A small notepad and pen were stuck to her fridge, and I took them over to the chair with me. It wasn't until I sat down that I even realized why I'd wanted them. For the first time in months, I put pen to paper and began to write.

Notes and words flowed out of me, and I edited as I went, scratching out things that didn't work and replaced them with new. I chased the music in my head, racing to capture everything that ran through my mind before it was too late.

My hand started to cramp at some point, but I pushed my way through it. It'd been too long since I'd written things out long-hand. Technology was wonderful for getting things down quickly and saving them in a place where they wouldn't get lost, but there was something to be said for the act of writing things out by hand.

At some point, I began humming the tune, making adjustments as I heard the various instruments in my head. Or rather, as I took out the different instruments. I was considered a solo artist, but I had a band that backed me with drums, bass, and a second guitar, sometimes giving me some assistance on vocals.

This song stripped away all of that. As it solidified in my head, I knew it would be only me and a guitar. Not acoustic, necessarily, but no frills. I didn't know if that sound would carry through an entire album, or a tour, but for this song, it worked.

Finally, I set down the pen and stared at the pages in front of me. It had been more than half a year since I'd written anything, and none of it had been this good. For a long time, writing had been exhausting, a chore. It had always been work, but anyone who did something difficult that they loved will tell you that there was a world of difference between satisfying hard work and the kind of thing you endured because it needed to be done.

I wasn't a fool, and I didn't believe in magical fixes or anything like that, but I did believe in inspiration, in the existence of something beyond what I could touch and see. I'd lost that, even before what had happened with Mitzi, but I'd found it again. And I didn't doubt for a moment why.

Paige hadn't only given me what I needed as a man and as a Dom. She'd given me back my voice.

TWENTY-EIGHT
PAIGE

Something had woken me up, but I didn't know what it was. For a moment, I was disoriented, wondering where I was, and then I felt the familiar comforter, saw the familiar shadows. I was home. But something still felt off. I stretched out my hand without really knowing why, but when I touched empty space, I remembered that I hadn't gone to bed alone.

I rolled onto my back again and sighed. I hadn't given much thought to whether or not Reb would stay the night, but I'd hoped he'd at least wake me up before he left rather than sneaking out. I didn't know what any of this meant. We hadn't made any declarations or commitments, so it was entirely possible that he simply hadn't felt like sleeping over, or maybe he thought it would've given the wrong impression. I'd understand that sort of hesitation, but I still wished he would've talked to me about it. I'd rather have had an awkward conversation than all of these questions.

I started to turn over, then stilled when I heard something. A faint noise. Not talking, exactly, and not loud enough for me to make out anything specific. It could have been the neighbor's television, but a glance at my phone told me that it was barely two o'clock in the morning. Mr. and Mrs. Armitage went to bed at eleven-thirty every night after they watched the news, and they got up at six-thirty every morning, whether they had anywhere to go or not. I knew this because they'd told me when I'd first met them. I was welcome to come over if I ever needed anything, but unless it was an emergency, I was never to disturb them between that eleven-thirty and six-thirty timeframe.

So why was I hearing what sounded like a radio?

No, not a radio.

Someone was singing.

No music, no commercials.

Just singing.

And it was coming from inside my apartment.

I blamed my still-fuzzy brain for taking so long to realize that it must've been Reb, though why he was singing in my living room, I couldn't figure out. I climbed out of bed and grabbed my robe from the back of my bathroom door. I didn't bother with anything else but headed out to the living room to see what was happening.

When I saw him sitting in my chair, I stopped, my curiosity getting the better of me. He held a few scraps of paper in one hand. The other rested on his knee, fingers tapping out a rhythm that went with the melody he was singing.

> *I thought I'd lost it all*
> *Would never trust again*
> *I tried to drown the pain*
> *And never let anyone in*

I didn't claim to know everything in Reb's discography, but I'd listened to a few songs. This didn't sound like anything he'd done before. It wasn't so much the style as it was the nature of it. Similar, maybe, to a song or two on his first album, but even they had notes of something I recognized now as loneliness. This one was passionate, full of longing, but hopeful too.

> *But I saw my future in your eyes*
> *Heard the song I thought was lost*
> *You brought me back to life*
> *Gave me my music once again*

His voice was raspier, rawer than what I'd heard on the albums, and I wondered if that was some sort of polishing done post-recording. I liked this one better.

I waited until he finished singing, until that last note faded away, and then I spoke, "That was amazing. When did you write it?"

"Just now," he said, turning to look at me. "I didn't mean to wake you."

I shook my head and crossed the space between us. It was a testament to how good his song was that it wasn't until now that I realized he wasn't wearing a shirt. "It wasn't a bad way to wake up."

He reached up and took my hand, tugging me down on his lap. I pulled my legs up and curled against his chest. I'd gotten this chair because I didn't have enough room for a couch, but I'd wanted something bigger than a regular chair. Fortunately, it was big enough to fit both of us. That should be a selling point.

"Everything okay?" I asked as I ran my fingers through his hair. "I know the bed's smaller than what you're used to–"

He caught my hand and brought it to his mouth, kissing my fingertips. "The bed's fine. I got up to use the bathroom, and then couldn't go back to sleep."

"Are you sure nothing's wrong?"

"Very." He slid his hand under my robe, curled his fingers around my calf. "I got inspired, and it's been a while, so I wanted to write it down before I lost it again." He nodded toward the paper he'd been holding when I first saw him. "I owe you a new notebook."

I smiled. "I'm sure I can come up with some way for you to pay me back."

He returned the smile as he leaned in for a kiss. His fingers tightened on my leg as I flicked my tongue against his lips. I moaned as his teeth scraped against my lip, the slight sting making heat coil in my stomach.

"It's because of you," he said as he rested his forehead

against mine. "That I was writing again. You helped me find the music."

I opened my mouth to protest, and he put a finger against my lips.

"You're my muse." He placed his palm on the side of my face. "I couldn't have done it without you."

"I didn't do anything."

"Yes, you did," he insisted. "You talked to Tanya, Sine, and Savannah, right? That's what they are to the guys. Their muses. And I never understood it. Until now."

I wasn't entirely sure I agreed with him, but I wasn't going to argue either. I wouldn't do anything to take away the joy I saw on his face, in his eyes. I kissed his forehead.

"You're worth it, you know." I traced his mouth with my fingers. "Worth the risk."

"I'm not going to make any crazy promises," he said. "Because I'm human. I know I'll do stupid shit that'll piss you off. But what I can promise is that I will never lie to you. Even when I do something stupid. I will never give you reason to doubt me." He took my face between his hands. "I swear it."

I maneuvered myself around until I was straddling his lap, our eyes locking. "I believe you."

His eyes slid down and then back up again. "How are you feeling?" His question was full of so much promise that it sent an immediate rush of arousal through me.

"A little sore," I admitted. I leaned closer and put my mouth against his ear. "But nothing that would keep me from wanting to ride you right now."

His eyes narrowed, and a shiver went down my spine. He reached for the belt on my robe, and I pulled back enough to let him untie it. My pulse was already racing as he wrapped his arms around me, but he ignored the fact that I was naked under my robe and instead pulled my arms behind my back. Without even looking, he quickly tied my wrists together and then leaned back in the chair.

I raised an eyebrow. "Not really what I was expecting."

He grinned at me. "Since I don't have access to all of my favorite toys, I figured I'd improvise."

His hands moved under my robe, pushing it off my shoulders until it caught on my bound hands. He made a sound of appreciation as his attention turned to my bared breasts.

"Now, my Paige, let's see how hot and bothered I can get you by playing with these pretty breasts of yours."

He slid his arm around my waist, his hand settling at the small of my back. He held me in place as he lowered his head, and the moment his tongue began to trace patterns on my skin, I was grateful for the steadying touch.

"Reb," I moaned.

"I love hearing you say my name like that." His lips tickled as he spoke. "In fact, I think the only words you're allowed to say now are my name, *please*, and *fuck*."

If my ass hadn't still been sensitive from getting spanked, I might have thought he was joking, but I wasn't about to risk it. I was fine with those three words.

Especially if he kept playing with my nipples like that. His fingers weren't only talented when it came to playing instruments. He could play me like no one else, rolling and pinching until every nerve was singing. And his mouth...*fuck*...the things this man could do with his mouth. His tongue teased the tip even as he wrapped his lips around it, and I writhed on his lap. I needed more.

"Please," I begged. "Please, Reb."

I pulled against my restraints, my actions more instinct than anything else. I wanted to bury my hands in his hair, hold his head in place. I hadn't realized just how frustrating it would be not being able to touch him when he could touch me.

"Such pretty nipples." His teeth scraped over one, then moved to the other, worrying at them until they were both throbbing.

"Fuck, Reb," I gasped. "I need–"

He made a tsking sound. "Those aren't any of your words, Paige."

I shivered, then cried out as he bit the side of my breast.

"I think maybe you need to be reminded who's in charge." His eyes glinted with the sort of light that made low things tighten. "What do you think?"

I swallowed hard, my body thrumming with need. "Please."

He moved one hand between us, opening his jeans. He wasn't wearing anything under them, and then his cock was out, thick and hard. His eyes locked with mine as he grabbed my hips.

"I want you on me, sweet Paige. You're going to ride

me until I come, and if you behave yourself while I'm emptying myself into that tight cunt of yours, I'll let you come too."

My pussy clenched, in part because of his words, the sort of coarse language I'd never thought of as a turn-on, but even if he hadn't said anything, I would've felt the need to have him inside me.

I nodded and let him guide me as I raised myself up on my knees. The tip of his cock brushed against me as he positioned me right where I needed to be. I didn't have my hands to balance me, but I trusted him to keep me from falling as I lowered myself onto him.

Every motion sent another ripple of pleasure through me. Every inch stretching me in ways that were still new. We weren't like puzzle pieces, perfectly interlocking, but rather like our bodies had been custom-made for each other. Each part of me molded around him until I couldn't tell where I ended and he began.

"Fuck, babe, I love being inside you," he groaned. His fingers flexed.

I wanted to tell him how amazing he felt. How I couldn't imagine ever finding anyone else who fit me this way. How I couldn't imagine wanting to. He was the only man I'd been with, and I didn't want to think about being with anyone else.

But he'd only given me three words, and I didn't want to disappoint him.

"Reb," I murmured his name as I kissed him. I loved the taste of him.

I rocked back and forth, putting the perfect amount of friction on my clit, the sensitive nerves there adding to the pressure in my belly.

"Don't come." He growled the order. "Not yet. Not until I say you can."

I nodded and shifted my weight so that the only stimulation I received was from me pushing up, then letting myself ease back down. It might have been enough to eventually reach climax, but right now, it was all about his pleasure. Not mine.

"Damn," he breathed. "Watching you bouncing on my cock like this. Those gorgeous tits of yours, that pussy squeezing me..." His grip on my hips tightened. "I want to mark you, my Paige. Not for punishment, but because I want you to always remember that you're mine." He yanked me toward him, giving me a brief, hard kiss. "You are mine, aren't you?"

I nodded, moving faster despite the burn in my legs. I needed him to come. My nails dug into my palms, and I fought to keep my balance. I'd never done this before, but I was pretty sure that it would've been easier with my hands untied.

He wrapped his arms around me, pulling me down hard enough to make stars spark behind my eyelids. He groaned my name as his cock pulsed inside of me, his mouth pressed against the side of my throat. I could feel him emptying himself inside me, and as his teeth scraped my skin, I spoke.

"Please, Reb," I whispered.

"You can come now," he said, the words muffled.

His thumb pressed against my clit, making hard, rough circles as he sucked on my neck, leaving the mark he'd wanted. The climax building inside me was stronger, more violent than anything I'd experienced before. It tore through me, and the last missing piece clicked into place, making me acknowledge what I'd already known.

I needed this as much as he did.

TWENTY-NINE
REB

I was tempted to stay in bed all day, and see how many ways I could make Paige scream my name. Unfortunately, she had to go to work, and she had far more willpower than I did. We left the apartment together but went in opposite directions when we reached the street.

The first thing I needed to do was get my new song written down before I forgot it. Besides, I figured I had enough time to do that before I went to see Chester. He wouldn't be up before the afternoon meeting we had scheduled anyway. I didn't see the point of waking him up, discussing things, and then having to re-explain them later.

I might as well get some work done while I waited.

As I settled into the small studio I'd set up at my place, I felt a fragment of fear grow. What if last night had been a fluke? I'd told Paige that she was my muse, and I'd meant it, but what if, despite the inspiration I'd experienced, I couldn't do it? What if it'd been too long? What if I'd already exhausted any talent I had?

I gave myself a shake, both mental and physical. I couldn't think like that. I *wouldn't* think like that. I'd written one song already, and even though some parts were rough, I knew it was good. And I had more in me. Nothing had solidified yet, but I could feel pieces of them in my head, and my intuition told me that they were better than anything I'd written before.

I went to work.

If I hadn't set the alarm on my phone, I probably would have worked right through my meeting. I'd completely lost myself in the process. Writing down notes, trying out different instruments, tweaking words until I found the exact right ones.

I would've preferred to keep going, but the things I had planned for today were important, and I'd accomplished a lot in the time I'd spent.

I made sure everything was saved, and then headed out, making a couple necessary calls. I lived close enough to the restaurant where we were scheduled to meet that it only took about twenty minutes to get there, but I was still ready to get things over and done with by the time we arrived.

"Mr. Union." The host was all smiles as he greeted me. "It's good to see you again."

I made small talk as best I could, not wanting to be rude to someone who'd only ever been nice to me, but I was still relieved when I reached the private room we used for our dinner meetings. When I stepped inside, three men were already there.

Chester had put on a wrinkled suit that looked at least five years out of fashion and was the ugliest shade of brown I'd ever seen. Not for the first time, I wondered what he spent his money on, because he sure as hell didn't use it to update his wardrobe. Then again, after seeing all the shit he'd had out for Mitzi, maybe it wasn't such a mystery after all.

On the opposite side of the table sat Roderick Leery and Trevor West, the first the VP of Solis Records, and the second his personal assistant. Both were smartly dressed, though Trevor's suit wasn't quite as expensive as Roderick's. I'd been working with these guys for years and respected them both, but we didn't have what I would've called a personal relationship. Still, I hoped they'd be on my side today.

I didn't bother with any of the usual niceties. "Chester's been supplying drugs for my ex-girlfriend, Mitzi, and probably giving the same stuff to roadies, other musicians, and who the hell knows else, although an investigation is beginning to uncover the depth of his deceit."

All three men stared at me for a moment, and then Chester laughed, a big, booming sound. A sound that I now recognized as fake.

"Come on, Reb, you know me. I don't mess with that shit." He glanced at the other men. "Sorry. That stuff."

I didn't waste my time arguing. I wasn't here for that. I was here to lay everything out on the table and get my life back on track. I pulled my phone out of my pocket and retrieved the video message I'd been sent a few minutes ago.

"Mitzi's on her way to rehab," I said and watched Chester begin to sweat, his face turning a deep, mottled red. "Courtesy of a deal made with the NYPD."

I held out my phone and let everyone watch as Mitzi sat down with a detective. I waited until she got a minute or so into her explanation of what she and Chester had done to me, then paused the video.

"I can send it to you if you'd like to see the rest, but I think we've run out of time to watch it just now." I glanced toward the door as I heard arguing coming from the main part of the restaurant. "And, by the way, Chester, if you haven't figured it out already, you're fired."

The door opened, and a pair of cops came through, followed by the detective Mitzi had been making her statement to. He went straight for Chester, already rattling off charges and Miranda rights.

I waited until the asshole had been escorted out before speaking again, mostly because his cursing and threats drowned out everything else. Roderick and Trevor hadn't said a word during the entire thing, and I got the impression that they were waiting for me to explain.

I didn't make them wait for long. "I didn't know what he was doing, but I should have. The past few months, I've been...out of it, to say the least. That's done. I'm ready to get back to work."

"That's good to know," Roderick said. He leaned

forward, his expression shrewd. "Do you want to wait until you have a new manager to discuss things?"

I shook my head. "I'll probably hire someone to handle the manager stuff, but I think we've been working together long enough to talk business ourselves."

I waited until he nodded and gestured at the chair across from him. I sat down, some of my tension easing. Getting Chester to answer for his crimes was only the first part of what I needed to do, and I'd been confident of how things would play out. In fact, I considered it fortunate that I hadn't gotten punched before the cops had come in. This next bit, however, I was less certain about.

"I've been writing again," I said. "And it's good...but not the same as anything I've done before. Similar to my first album, but different enough that some people aren't going to like it."

Roderick nodded slowly. "Your deadlines are coming up fast. Will you be able to meet them?"

I considered the question before answering, "I think so, but only with these new songs. I don't know if I could get you the sort of stuff I did before."

Roderick looked over at his assistant who'd been sitting quietly, taking notes. "What do you think?"

"I think, after the last few months, people will respond better to something new than they would to the same thing," Trevor answered with a half-smile. "After the community service you've been doing, they'll think of it as part of your new image."

That was closer to the truth than he realized. Paige was

responsible for both my image and my music, though I knew she'd say she was just showing people who I really was, that I'd always had the music in me.

And the sooner I finished here, the sooner I could make sure she knew how I felt about her.

THIRTY

PAIGE

Damn traffic. I was supposed to meet Reb at The Kamden McBride Foundation ten minutes ago. He hadn't told me details about what he planned to do before, but he had said that he was going to do some of his own work on his new image.

I pressed my hands against my stomach, hoping to calm the butterflies fluttering there. Just the thought of seeing him again had my body reacting like I hadn't been with him just last night. I knew some people may have written it off as merely something physical. My first taste of sex had been a pleasurable experience. Of course, I'd want more.

And I did.

But it wasn't only that.

What I felt was too fast, too soon, but I couldn't control it.

As my taxi pulled up to the building, I pushed aside everything I was feeling and focused on the work we were about to do. I had to take things one day at a time with Reb.

He was already there when I arrived, and I took a moment to watch him with a pair of kids who were here for family day. He was so good with them. We hadn't talked about kids or marriage or anything permanent, and a few weeks ago, I would've laughed if anyone had talked about thinking of a future with someone they'd only known for such a short time, but it was so easy to picture him playing with his own kids.

With *our* kids.

Fuck.

I took a steadying breath and started toward him. He turned before I reached him, his entire face lighting up. He wrapped his arms around me, lifting me up so he could kiss me. He kept it chaste but didn't put me down when he broke the kiss.

"I know this isn't the most romantic time or place, but I can't wait any longer." His expression was serious. "I love you, my Paige."

REB'S TIMING hadn't gotten any better since the night he told me how he felt.

The eight of us had spent the last few days in Aspen, at the home Reb and his friends shared, and it had been amazing. The other women and I had gone shopping while

Reb pitched music to Erik for the movie of his new book, and Jace worked with Alix on the cover, then we'd all come together for dinner and movies or skiing. The first night we were all there, we'd decorated the house for Christmas, and last night, we'd done gift exchanges. Today, the other couples had headed to where they'd be spending Christmas, leaving Reb and me alone for the holiday.

Which meant, tonight, we were using the playroom.

Over the past three months, Reb had been introducing me to various aspects of the BDSM lifestyle. At first, he'd made it gradual, still concerned about scaring me off, but then I'd bought him a flogger for his birthday and things had taken off from there.

He'd used that same flogger earlier tonight, and my ass was still smarting, but it wasn't at the top of the sensations I was feeling at the moment.

My arms were stretched above my head, the handcuffs around my wrists attached to the chain hanging from the ceiling. A pair of matching silver clamps were attached to my nipples, the chain connecting them to each other. One day, he'd promised to add a third clip for my clit, but I wasn't quite ready for that yet. The fact that I currently had a thin plastic shaft in my ass, and Reb's cock in my pussy, was more than enough for now.

He'd been making these insanely deep, slow strokes, telling me about all the ways he was going to fuck me, all the places we were going to have sex...and I'd been pleading with him to just let me come.

Then, he'd said the words that proved he had the worst

sense of timing of anyone I'd ever met.

"Marry me, my Paige."

Time stopped.

"What?"

He pushed himself deep inside me and slid one hand down between my legs. The other, he moved from my waist up to the chain resting just below my breasts. He gave it a little tug, and I let out a gasp.

"I said, *marry me, my Paige*."

I turned my head slightly to look at him behind me. "Are you really asking me that now? Like this?"

He chuckled and rotated his hips, sending a ripple of pleasure through me. "I meant to ask you somewhere more romantic, but I couldn't wait any longer."

His fingers began to move over my swollen clit, and I shuddered. I was so close to coming, and he knew exactly how to keep me right on the edge.

"Should I make you wait until you accept my proposal to let you come?"

I whimpered, and he put his mouth against my ear.

"Don't worry, Paige, I wouldn't do that to you. You may come."

He pulled back, paused for a moment, and then drove into me, hard. I cried out, the combination of overwhelming sensations tipping me over into the sort of orgasm that made my vision go white and my entire body quiver. And then he came too, growling out a declaration of love.

It wasn't until he was releasing my restraints, removing

the clamps, and doing all the things that a Dom did to take care of his sub, that I gave him his answer.

"Yes."

He appeared to have stopped breathing. "Can you say that again?"

I smiled and put a hand on his cheek. "Yes, Reb, I'll marry you."

With a laugh, he swept me into his arms and spun me around, singing the first song he'd written for me. My head whirled, and I knew this is what life with him would always be. Full of laughter and love...and music.

THE END

WOW!!! I hope you've enjoyed reading the Billionaire's Muse series as much as I did writing it. As a special treat, I'm writing a bonus novella, Change of Plans (The Billionaire's Muse – The Wedding). I'm not telling who's wedding we'll attend, but everybody will be there, so be sure you are signed up to my newsletter and I'll email the ebook to you for free, TWO WEEKS BEFORE the official release on Amazon on Valentine's day. You can sign up at www.msparker.com/newsletter

M. S. Parker

ALSO BY M. S. PARKER

The Billionaire's Muse

Bound

One Night Only

Damage Control

Take Me, Sir

Make Me Yours

The Billionaire's Sub

The Billionaire's Mistress

Con Man Box Set

HERO Box Set

A Legal Affair Box Set

The Client

Indecent Encounter

Dom X Box Set

Unlawful Attraction Box Set

Chasing Perfection Box Set

Blindfold Box Set

Club Prive Box Set

The Pleasure Series Box Set

Exotic Desires Box Set

Pure Lust Box Set

Casual Encounter Box Set

Sinful Desires Box Set

Twisted Affair Box Set

Serving HIM Box Set

ABOUT THE AUTHOR

M. S. Parker is a USA Today Bestselling author and the author of the Erotic Romance series, Club Privè and Chasing Perfection.

Living in Las Vegas, she enjoys sitting by the pool with her laptop writing on her next spicy romance.

Growing up all she wanted to be was a dancer, actor or author. So far only the latter has come true but M. S. Parker hasn't retired her dancing shoes just yet. She is still waiting for the call for her to appear on Dancing With The Stars.

When M. S. isn't writing, she can usually be found reading– oops, scratch that! She is always writing.

For more information:
www.msparker.com
msparkerbooks@gmail.com

ACKNOWLEDGMENTS

First, I would like to thank all of my readers. Without you, my books would not exist. I truly appreciate each and every one of you.

A big "thanks" goes out to all the Facebook fans, street team, beta readers, and advanced reviewers. You are a HUGE part of the success of all my series.

I have to thank my PA, Shannon Hunt. Without you my life would be a complete and utter mess. Also a big thank you goes out to my editor Lynette and my wonderful cover designer, Sinisa. You make my ideas and writing look so good.

Made in the USA
Monee, IL
25 March 2021